WRONG EXIT

N. L. HINKENS

Text copyright @ 2022 Norma Hinkens

Published by Dunecadia Publishing, California

ISBN: 978-1-947890-34-3

Cover by: **www.derangeddoctordesign.com**

Editing by: **www.jeanette-morris.com/first-impressions-writing**

DEDICATION

For Alana, who traveled 3,000 miles with me.

1

___

I've never won anything in my life before—not even as much as a lousy scratch off lottery ticket or a cheesy game at a baby shower. I just don't have that kind of luck. I've had to work hard for everything I have. Which makes the letter I'm holding in my hand all the more remarkable.

I trace my finger over the embossed legal letterhead, admiring the luxury of the thick cream paper as I ponder the words for the umpteenth time.

THIS IS formal notice that the decedent, Wilhelmina Elizabeth Cleary, died on March 31, 2022, and that you, Cora Helena Lewis, have been named the sole beneficiary of the real property located at 2517 Forest Hill Avenue, Katonah, New York, included in her estate.

. . .

A COPY of the Inventory and Final Accounting for the above-referenced estate is enclosed. Please contact me at (212) 621-1916 at your earliest convenience to discuss the claims process.

SINCERELY,
>   Maxwell Gutfeld
>   Attorney at Law

WILHELMINA ELIZABETH CLEARY was an eccentric recluse, estranged from her only daughter. She was also my maternal grandmother.

I never met her.

2

_____

"**A**re you really going through with this?" Clay asks, folding his arms in front of his chest as he leans against the doorframe.

"That's what it looks like," I quip, tucking a rolled T-shirt into the side pocket of my suitcase lying open on the bed. I turn to peer at my husband over my shoulder and flash him a grin. "I am coming back, you know. You're acting like we're separating or something before we've even had a chance to celebrate our first wedding anniversary."

Clay makes a disgruntled sound. "I just don't like the thought of you driving clear across the country. It's a forty-two-hour trek from Los Angeles to Katonah. What if your car breaks down in the middle of the desert? You can't so much as change a flat tire. There are crazy people out there nowadays who'd be only too happy to take advantage of you. Let's face it, Cora, you're not exactly savvy when it comes to reading dangerous situations. You're far too trusting."

"Which is why I've invited Adele to come with me," I remind him. "We're going to share the driving, and between the two of us, I'm sure we can figure out any problems that spring up along the way."

A dark frown creases Clay's forehead. "That doesn't give me any peace of mind. Adele's no better equipped than you to handle a three-thousand-mile trip. She's a terrible driver. She's had two wrecks in the past year alone—maybe more, for all I know."

"If you could call them that," I retort. "She barely touched that Audi's bumper in the parking lot, and the only reason she rear-ended a truck was because of the wild turkeys crossing the road. There was nothing she could do about it. Everyone was slamming on their brakes."

Clay lets out a peeved sigh as I flip the lid of my half-filled suitcase closed. He knows it's hopeless trying to dissuade me once I've made up my mind about something. Stubbornness runs in my veins. He's already tried talking me into flying to New York instead of driving. Not in a million years, after my last disastrous flight. I had a full-blown panic attack, and the pilot was almost forced to divert the plane. I'm done with flying, and I'm pretty sure the airline's done with me.

"Honey," I say, reverting to a cajoling tone, "I know you wish you were coming with me, and believe me, I wish you were too. But this is your busy time of year at work, and you said yourself you have to study for your upcoming CPA exam. I don't want to wait until the middle of June to leave. Maxwell advised me to put the house on the market before the summer season kicks off."

I step toward him and wrap my arms around his neck to assuage the nagging guilt in my gut. Clay's complained in the past that I neglect him, although he seems to have resigned himself to my hectic schedule. My job as a fashion blogger consumes every waking hour, and I'm gone a lot to trade shows on the weekends. But it also allows me the kind of flexibility he can only dream of in his accounting career. "You do realize this is going to change everything for us," I say. "We can move out of this chicken crate apartment and buy a home of our own. We'll be mortgage free after only three months of marriage, thanks to my fairy grandmother. What young couple gets to enjoy that level of freedom?"

I stretch up on my tiptoes and plant a kiss on his lips. "I need to get going. I'm meeting Adele at the mall to do some last-minute shopping for our trip."

A look of alarm crosses Clay's face. "Don't go spending money you don't have yet. If the will's contested, it could be years before you see a penny of it."

"You mean money *we* don't have," I correct him, wagging a finger in jest. "We're married so it's *our* money, as far as I'm concerned. Don't worry. Adele and I are planning on doing this trip on a budget. I won't believe my grandmother's house is actually mine until I get to New York and see it for myself. And I don't intend to spend the proceeds until the money from the sale is safely lodged in our bank account."

On the drive to the Towne Center Mall, I go over in my mind the phone conversation I had with Maxwell Gutfeld the day after I received his letter. He was the consummate legal professional, expressing his affection for my late grandmother, and his condolences for my loss. I didn't bother pointing out that it wasn't all that great a loss as I'd never actually met her—or even talked with her. When my mother fell pregnant with me at nineteen, she and my grandmother had a falling out and never spoke again. Any time I pressed my mother on the issue, she always said she wanted to spare me the details. As best I could gather, she refused to marry my father and left Katonah one night shortly afterward without telling anyone where she was going.

When my mother was dying of cancer four years ago, she expressed some regret that she hadn't tried to reach out to my grandmother and repair their relationship. She felt she'd been too harsh with her, and they'd both been too stubborn. She even urged me to try to contact her after she was gone. But people always say that kind of thing at the end of their lives, so I didn't give it a second thought. I had no desire to track down the woman who'd essentially kicked us to the curb when we needed her most. Evidently, in the end, she'd had some regrets about leaving her pregnant daughter without a roof over her head. I guess I'm the lucky recipient of her remorse. When Maxwell divulged that my grandmother's property was valued at a little over a million dollars, I could scarcely take it in. It blew my mind that she would leave such a windfall to someone she knew absolutely nothing about. I could have been a heroin addict, for all she knew.

Inside the mall, I spot Adele sitting on a bench hunched over her phone, her thick chestnut hair tumbling over her shoulders. An affectionate smile spreads across my face as I approach her. Adele and I have been best friends since elementary school, and we do everything together—*did* everything together—until I got married. She was with me the night I met Clay, and she was maid of honor at our wedding. But we haven't kept in touch much, of late. My burgeoning fashion blog is beginning to attract some big-league advertisers, which is a dream come true for me, but it doesn't leave me with a lot of extra time. This trip will be a chance for us to reconnect and catch up on things. Adele was hesitant when I first broached the idea of her accompanying me to New York on a road trip. Her seventeen-year-old brother, Jackson, has been getting into more and more serious trouble, and her parents put a lot of pressure on her to fix his messes. She's the only one who can get through to him. I figured she could use a break from the never-ending drama, so I got to work plotting out the road trip on a travel app I downloaded. Then, I sold the idea to her with over-the-top enthusiasm. "It will be our very own Thelma-and-Louise adventure—without the illegal parts of course," I said, with a wink. "The kind of road trip we'll tell our grandkids about one day."

Adele's a huge country music fan, so when I told her we'd be spending a night or two in Nashville, she finally caved. It probably didn't hurt that I assured her I would be paying for the trip in full. Adele doesn't earn great money at her administrative job in a warehouse—I know because I used to work there too, until my blog started making money. Clay asked me outright if I was going to finance the entire trip for Adele, and I kind of blew him off. He's worried about me maxing out the credit cards and then discovering there's some kind of legal issue with my inheritance when I arrive in New York. I'm not concerned. After talking to Maxwell, I'm confident everything's above board, and it's only a matter of me showing up with my ID and signing on the dotted line.

"Hey you!" I call out to Adele as I draw near to where she's sitting.

She glances up and grins before jumping to her feet. "I can't believe we're doing this," she laughs in a breathless whisper, as we embrace. "I feel almost guilty—like we're running away together or something."

"Wouldn't be the first time," I reply with a chuckle. "Remember when we were eleven and we stuffed our blankets and pillows into our overnight bags and made a pact to run away because our lousy parents wouldn't let us go to Jason's birthday party sleepover?"

Adele rolls her eyes. "Yeah, we decided to sleep on a park bench. We didn't make for the most creative runaways, did we? I think we lasted until eight o'clock before your fear of the dark and my chattering teeth sent us skedaddling home."

I link my arm through hers as we stroll through the mall. "Only to discover that your dad had been watching us at the park the whole time from the warmth of his truck."

Adele gives a thoughtful nod. "There won't be anyone watching over us this time. I just hope we don't have any car trouble. I don't know the first thing about jump-starting an engine. I have a hard time jump-starting myself in the mornings."

"It's 2022. And there's such a thing as cell phones and credit cards," I remind her. "And we won't be alone. We'll be on the I-40 with thousands of other vehicles."

"Except when we take all those detours to look at weird stuff off the beaten track—Cadillac Ranch and the like," Adele responds.

"Quit being such a worrywart!" I laugh, squeezing her arm playfully. "It's time you threw caution to the wind and let your hair down a little."

She shrugs. "It's a long way, that's all. I've never even been to most of the states we'll be driving through. I don't want to end up getting lost in the middle of nowhere. Neither of us are much good at directions."

"We're not going to get lost. And if we do end up taking a

wrong exit, Señorita Siri will be all over us in a heartbeat." I grin across at her. "Recalculating ... recalculating ... recalculating."

Adele flinches, a disquieted look in her eyes. "Let's hope that's not the last word we ever hear."

3

"Well, I guess this is it," I say, with a tingle of excitement as I hug Clay goodbye. I reach for my bulging suitcase, packed to the hilt with the new purchases I made at the mall last week using the credit cards I promised not to max out. "I'll be back in a couple of weeks, a million dollars richer, on paper, at least. Hopefully, my grandmother's place sells quickly so we can go house hunting for a new home with a pool before summer."

"Be careful," Clay says in a husky voice, brushing a kiss on my forehead. He turns to Adele who's hovering impatiently in the doorway, dressed in brand new denim cutoff shorts and a teal halter top that flatters her in all the right places. "Look after my wife," he warns, giving her a loaded look.

I'm taken aback by the edge in his tone. Ordinarily, he gets along just fine with Adele, but he hasn't quite forgiven her, yet, for agreeing to accompany me. Over lunch at the mall last week, Adele shared with me that he'd pleaded with her, on more than one occasion, to try and talk me out of the road trip. He wanted me to wait until after he'd taken his CPA exam so he could drive out there with me. But I'm not waiting another two months. I want to buy a home as soon as possible so that we can start a family.

"I'll check in with you every night and give you the scoop on our adventures," I call to him over my shoulder, as Adele and I head out to the Tahoe parked in the driveway—a wedding present from Clay's parents. They made a point of letting us know how many car seats it could accommodate when they handed us the keys at our wedding reception. No pressure! I'm totally up for being a young mom, but Clay keeps saying we can't afford it—not that money will be a problem anymore.

Adele and I have packed so much stuff in the back of the Tahoe, it looks like we're moving. Clay doesn't understand why we need to bring our own pillows, but I'm a bit like Goldilocks when it comes to hotel pillows—too hard, too lumpy, too flat. Ten days is a long time to be away from the comfort of my own bed.

At the last minute, I even decided to throw in a couple of sleeping bags in case Adele and I are ever caught in a situation when we need them. I've never camped in my life but, if it comes down to it, sleeping in the SUV will add another element of excitement to our adventure. Of course, we had to pack a generous selection of clothing and footwear for all types of weather as neither of us has any idea what to expect. We Googled late spring Midwest weather, but for a pair of fashionistas like ourselves, the range of projected temperatures was enough to justify bringing half our wardrobes, in addition to the new outfits we purchased last week. I intend to blog my way across the country and I can't be seen on Instagram wearing the same thing twice.

Starting up the engine, I grin deliriously across at Adele

and break into a woefully off-key rendition of *New York, New York*. We burst out laughing, and then Adele cuts off abruptly and nudges me in the ribs. "Better wave to your hubby one last time," she mutters, with a subtle tilt of her head toward the front door where Clay is standing with hunched shoulders, hands stuffed in his pockets, waiting for us to pull out. "He looks like an overgrown kid who's just found out there's no Santa."

I suppress another fit of the giggles as I wave at Clay, trying to look suitably dejected at the thought of leaving him behind. It will be the longest we've been apart since we got married, but I aim to make the most of this opportunity. With our jobs being as demanding as they are, we only took a three-day honeymoon, so I deserve to have a little fun now that we'll have more than enough money to be comfortable for the foreseeable future. We won't have a mortgage to worry about either, so he might even agree to starting a family sooner than we'd planned.

I toot the horn as I turn the corner, breathing out a sigh of relief. "Awkward goodbye—check. All right, let's get this party started. You're in charge of music."

Adele reaches for my phone and taps a ballerina-shaped fingernail on the screen to open the Spotify road-trip playlist we created together over a few glasses of wine a few nights ago. She syncs my phone to the car stereo with an impish grin. "Okay, kicking it off with *Go Your Own Way* by Fleetwood Mac," she announces, already swaying in her seat to the music.

We enter the I-10 on-ramp singing at the top of our lungs, high on a potent cocktail of adrenalin, caffeine, and Californian sunshine. I'm ecstatic at the thought of spending the next ten days with my best friend. I've let our relationship slide over the past few months, but thankfully,

Adele hasn't been weird about it. She likes Clay and she's happy for me. It's only a matter of time before she meets her own Mr. Right, and when she does, I intend to be there for her just like she's been there for me.

"What's our first stop?" I ask, tapping my fingers on the steering wheel to the beat of the music.

Adele frowns down at her phone. "Kingman, Arizona. We'll hit the museum there. It wouldn't be right to set out across the legendary Route 66 without educating ourselves about it. In fact, why don't we start right now?" She scrolls on her screen for a moment, then shoots me a triumphant look. "Here we go: *Six things you may not know about Route 66.*"

"Ugh! Don't read me a bunch of facts and figures. I'm a visual learner."

"This is interesting," Adele continues, unabated. "Did you know that Route 66 crosses eight states and three time zones?"

I groan. "Technically, that's facts and figures. Got anything more exciting?"

"Hmm ... oh wow, check this out. It says here that James and Utha Marie Welch were murdered along Route 66 while they slept in their car after passing on a motel room because it was too expensive." Adele turns to me, a look of horror seared on her face. "No sleepovers in the Tahoe for me."

"Don't worry, it's strictly glamping for us L.A. girls," I assure her. "How long until we get to Kingman?"

"It's a five-hour drive. I'll be starving by then."

I gesture to the cooler and grocery bags filled with snacks behind our seats. "It's not like you didn't bring enough food to last the entire trip."

"I need real food to preserve my figure," Adele says,

wiggling her hands suggestively over her perfectly proportioned curves.

I roll my eyes. "Fine, we'll get lunch in Kingman before we hit the museum. Then it's off to the Grand Canyon, right?"

Adele nods. "I'm still reeling from the price of hotels there."

"We could always resort to sleeping in the car," I say, with a mischievous wink. "We'd just have to watch out for the serial killers and bears."

"No camping!" We blurt out in unison before dissolving into laughter.

"I'm looking forward to a dip in the hotel pool after driving all day," I say. "It's going to be hot later—a high of eighty-six in Kingman."

"Yikes!" Adele reaches for her water and takes a hasty sip. "Are you sure you don't want to take a helicopter ride at the Grand Canyon?" she asks, in a wistful tone. She holds her phone up to me, and I chance a glance across at the bright red helicopter on the screen.

"Not going to happen," I reply firmly. "We can drive the scenic route of the south rim to the Desert View overlook instead. It's supposed to be stunning."

Adele shrugs. "You can see so much more from a helicopter."

I bite back my irritation. I realize she's disappointed, but she should know better than to push it. "Look, even if I wasn't terrified of all things airborne—including winged insects—the helicopter ride's too expensive. We're doing this trip on a budget," I remind her. "Fingers crossed, everything goes smoothly, and my grandmother's place sells quickly. But Clay and I will need every penny of that money to buy a home in Los Angeles."

Adele throws me a sideways glance as she twists a strand of hair around her finger. "You're so lucky. Are you curious to find out more about your grandmother when you go through her photo albums and stuff?"

I twist my lips, trying to quash the resentment that rises to the surface at the thought. I've been keeping my emotions in check by handling this like a business transaction. There was a time I would have loved to have known more about my grandmother. But it's the old adage—too little, too late. I'm grateful for the financial windfall, but I would trade it in a heartbeat for a grandmother who'd cared about me all these years.

I always felt guilty knowing that my mother struggled to raise me on her own. As a result, I came to the conclusion long ago that my grandmother probably wasn't worth knowing. Even if she couldn't get past her anger at my mother, she could have made an effort to reach out to me, at some point. As a child, I couldn't understand why she never showed up on Grandparent's Day at school, or for birthday parties, or any holiday, for that matter. It was easier to tell the kids at school that she was dead. I suppose I could have gone for wheelchair-bound, but then I'd still have had to explain why she never sent me Christmas presents or called to wish me Happy Birthday.

"I don't see the point in getting to know her now that she's gone," I say, hoping my tone signals the end of the conversation.

Adele skewers me with a shrewd look. "You never know what you might find out."

Two-and-a-half hours later, we exit the highway at Barstow in search of a restroom.

"I'm going to gas up while we're here," I say, as we cruise down Main Street. "We can use the restroom at the gas station."

Adele pulls a face. "Not my first choice. They have outlet stores here somewhere. We should check them out. They're bound to have cleaner restrooms, and we could do a little shopping while we're there."

I shoot her a look of disbelief. "Seriously? We're not stopping at some lame outlet mall in the middle of nowhere when we live in mall utopia."

Adele raises her hands in a placating gesture. "Point taken. Just trying to circumvent the dreaded gas station pit stop."

Moments later, I spot a Chevron station and pull in. It's crowded, but I manage to snag an open pump after a minivan pulls out. "You go first," I say to Adele, as I climb out of the car. "I'll gas up."

As the price on the pump ticks steadily upward, I glance around curiously at the other patrons. A frail-looking elderly woman peers out through the window of a dark blue Cadillac as her stooped husband struggles with his credit card at the pump. Next to them, a roofing contractor jabbers on his phone while he unscrews the cap on the tank of his work truck. A Dodge camper truck in dire need of a wash idles in line behind him. In the driver's seat, an angry-looking young man in a baseball cap and sunglasses is mindlessly chewing gum, one elbow resting on the open window. A young woman with long dark hair slouches on the passenger seat next to him, head bent as though she's asleep or looking at something in her lap.

I finish filling my tank and pull over into a parking spot on the far side of the gas station, out of the way of traffic. I climb out and stand in the shade while I try calling Clay. He texts me back almost immediately that he's in a meeting and can't talk. I send him a heart Emoji and slip my phone back into my pocket, just as the elderly man who was fumbling with his credit card moments earlier, collapses by the Cadillac. My heart jolts in my chest. I hesitate only for a second, before dashing to his side and dropping to my knees next to him. He's conscious, but babbling incoherently. I'm not sure if it's heat stroke or if he's had a heart attack. "Call an ambulance!" I yell to anyone within earshot, as I cradle his liver-spotted head in my arms to help him breathe more easily.

"Sir, you're going to be all right," I soothe, as the man's rheumy eyes blink uncomprehendingly up at me. "Help's on the way."

All of a sudden, I notice the elderly woman who was sitting in the Cadillac hovering over me, leaning on the car for support. "Harold, I'm right here," she squeezes out through pale, wrinkled lips.

"She's shaking," I say to the contractor who's on the phone with the emergency services. "Can you help her get back in her car? It's not going to do any good if she ends up on the ground too."

"An ambulance is on the way, ma'am," he assures her, as he guides her back to her seat.

Moments later, an employee comes running out to see what all the commotion is about. "What happened? Is he okay?" the man asks, rubbing an agitated hand over his glistening bald head as he surveys the situation.

"He's conscious," I reply. "Someone called for an ambulance. He might be dehydrated."

The man gives an uncertain nod. "I'll fetch some ice water," he says, before disappearing back inside.

Adele returns from the bathroom and hurries over to me. "What's going on? Is he all right?" she whispers.

"I'm not sure. He keeled over when he was filling up," I explain. "It might have been the heat. The ambulance is on its way."

Adele sucks on her bottom lip. "I can wait with him if you want to use the restroom."

I shake my head. "I don't want to leave him until the ambulance gets here." Adrenalin has flooded my system and erased my need for anything other than to get this elderly man help. He's confused and scared enough as it is without me abandoning him to the arms of another stranger.

Relief washes over me when the welcome wail of emergency service vehicles reaches my ears. An ambulance veers into the gas station, lights flashing, tailed by two police cruisers. I gratefully release the man into the care of the paramedics who squat down next to him, life-saving equipment at hand. They rattle off a series of questions, none of which I can answer, and most of which only seem to confuse his elderly wife. I don't know if it's shock or dementia, but, clearly, she's in no condition to drive. The police are already making arrangements to transport her to the hospital and take the Cadillac home for her. Minutes later, the ambulance exits the Chevron station, and I make a mad dash inside to use the bathroom.

"That wasn't exactly the memorable first stop of our trip I was hoping for," I remark to Adele, as we get back on the I-40.

"It could have been worse. At least he didn't die," she answers.

A shudder crosses my shoulders at the depressing thought. A death on the first day of our road trip—or any day of it, for that matter—would be enough to cast a permanent shadow over the idea of regaling our grandkids with our cross-country adventure.

Adele throws me a contrite look. "Sorry, that came out as more of a downer than I intended. What I meant was that you were awesome back there. You saved that old man's life. We should be celebrating, not moping." She cranks up the music and, before long, our mood has lifted and we're bopping along to *On The Road Again* by Willie Nelson.

A little over three hours later, we pull off at Kingman ready to hit the first planned stop of our trip.

"My stomach's rumbling," Adele says. "How about we grab lunch first and then check out the museum?"

"I won't argue with that," I say. "I'm famished too—that adrenalin rush earlier depleted all my reserves."

We drive downtown until we come across an old sixties-style diner with the perfect facade for taking Route 66 fashion selfies for my Instagram account.

"Now, this is how I imagined Route 66," I say, grinning across at Adele who's busy snapping pictures as we pull into the parking lot.

I reach into the back of the Tahoe for my purse and freeze when my fingers tangle with human hair.

4

A scream cements itself in my throat as a young woman emerges like a hermit crab from beneath our sleeping bags. Her red-rimmed eyes peer up at me from under her dark, tousled hair. Despite her disheveled appearance, and thin frame, her clothes appear to be in decent shape, and I don't detect any body odor emanating from her, so I'm guessing she isn't homeless. I glance across at Adele who's halfway twisted around in her seat, one hand clapped over her mouth, eyes bulging in disbelief.

My mind races as I try to piece together how this woman ended up in my Tahoe. She must have climbed in at the gas station in Barstow while we were distracted with the medical emergency. A prickling feeling crosses my shoulders like a caterpillar tread. It's beyond disturbing to think that a stranger has been buried beneath our belongings in the back of my car for several hours, unbeknownst to Adele or me. It feels like a violation of sacred space. The dangers Clay warned me about were supposed to be out on the road, or in dodgy campsites, not inside the air-conditioned sanctuary of my own vehicle. My heart races up my throat when I consider the fact that this woman could easily have stabbed Adele or me in the neck, or strangled us with a piece of wire, or put a bullet in us, for that matter.

As the shock begins to settle, my thoughts move in a more compassionate direction. She didn't harm us, so, obviously, she had some reason other than ill-intent for hitching a covert ride. She could be in trouble. Whatever her story is, she was desperate enough to take a chance on climbing into a stranger's car. She likely weighed her options at the Chevron station and decided the odds would be in her favor with two young women.

"Who ... who are you?" I manage to stammer at last.

"Gianna." She sniffs against her sleeve, looking at me expectantly.

"I'm Cora," I reply. "This is my friend, Adele."

"I'm sorry for scaring you like that," Gianna says. "I ... I had to get out of Barstow. When I saw all the stuff in the back of your car, I figured I could hide beneath it."

"Who exactly are you hiding from?" Adele asks, finally finding her voice.

"My boyfriend." A shadow flits across Gianna's face. "He's ... dangerous."

I frown as an image of the dirty Dodge camper truck at the gas station with its angry-looking driver comes to mind. He looked like the kind of man you wouldn't want to cross. Is this the same girl who was sitting hunched over in the passenger seat next to him? I chew on the inside of my mouth as I throw a nervous glance around the diner parking lot. The last thing Adele and I need is an unhinged boyfriend chasing us down. He looked like the type who would keep a gun duct taped beneath the seat of his truck.

"Was that your boyfriend in the camper truck at the

Chevron station?" I ask, dreading her answer but needing to confirm my suspicion.

Gianna nods weakly and draws her knees up to her chest. "I told CJ to get out and help that old man, but he just kept filming him. He thought the whole thing was funny. He even uploaded it to Snapchat. After the ambulance arrived, he went inside to buy us breakfast. I saw my chance to get away and hid in your car while you were talking to the paramedics."

I rub the back of my hand distractedly. I'm still trying to take it all in. It's not every day a stranger stows away in the back of my car. I'm not sure if I believe Gianna's story—if that's even her real name. I don't feel comfortable prying into her relationship with her boyfriend, but I suppose I have the right to, as she more or less broke into my car. She said he was dangerous, so I assume he was abusing her. Maybe he was even taking her somewhere against her will —she certainly didn't look too happy sitting in the truck. Whatever the case, she has inadvertently become my problem.

Another thought occurs to me, making me break out in a cold sweat. What if she's a minor? If CJ called the police to report her missing, I could be accused of kidnapping her. There's no guarantee she wouldn't side with him if it came down to it, like abused women—driven by fear—sometimes do. "How old are you?" I ask.

She blinks at me, injecting a pause into her answer that immediately raises a red flag. "Nineteen."

I exchange a loaded glance with Adele. Judging by the flicker of suspicion in her eyes, she didn't miss the hesitation either. My heart tightens in my chest.

"Do you have any ID on you?" Adele asks.

Gianna's face falls. "You ... don't believe me?"

Adele shrugs. "We need to be sure. Look at it from our point of view. You're a stranger who crawled into our car without our knowledge. How are we supposed to know if you're telling us the truth?"

Gianna sighs. "CJ has my ID. He only lets me have it if I absolutely need it."

"How convenient!" Adele snaps, folding her arms. I can sense her resistance to our intruder building by the minute.

"You're an adult. Why do you let him do that?" I chime in.

Gianna hikes one shoulder in a pathetic shrug. "You don't understand. It's ... complicated."

"Tell me about it," I say, dragging my fingers through my hair. "I'm still trying to wrap my head around it. Adele and I were on an idyllic road trip until, suddenly, we discover we've been unwittingly transporting a stranger fleeing an abusive relationship. It's like a crime show special." I let out a heavy sigh, eying the diner door longingly through the car window. "I'm starving. How about we go inside and talk about this over lunch? You must be hungry too if you didn't get any breakfast."

Gianna shoots me a chagrined look. "I ... don't have any money. I grabbed my backpack out of the truck but—"

"Let me guess," Adele cuts her off. "CJ has your wallet too."

Gianna's lip quivers.

I catch Adele's eye and give a subtle shake of my head. Gianna seems fragile enough as it is without berating her about the situation she's in.

"Don't worry about the money," I assure her. "Lunch is on me."

After checking twice to make sure my car is locked this time, I head inside the diner with Adele and Gianna. My nerves are rattled at the thought of CJ possibly following us, so I request a table next to the window to keep a close eye on the Tahoe. The minute the hostess seats us, Gianna excuses herself and heads to the restroom, her black backpack slung over one shoulder.

Adele places her elbows on the table and leans across it. "Can you believe this? We haven't even made it to the Grand Canyon, and you've already saved the life of a senior citizen and rescued a teenage runaway. Talk about a trip to capture the grandkids' imaginations!" She hesitates and casts a glance in the direction Gianna disappeared in. "I don't believe for one minute she's nineteen. We need to take her to a shelter or something after this."

I nod in agreement. "Let's get her fed and calmed down first and then we'll make a plan."

"Heads up! She's on her way back," Adele murmurs, leaning back in her seat and pretending to stretch.

"Feeling better?" I ask, smiling at Gianna as she rejoins us. She's taken the trouble to comb out her long hair and wash her face. Her skin's still a little blotchy from crying, but she's an attractive girl. She could pass for anywhere from sixteen to twenty. That alone is reason enough for me not to get talked into giving her a ride anywhere after lunch, other than to a shelter or the police station. I'm fairly certain she was in the Dodge camper truck at Barstow, but I don't know how much of what else she told us is true. Her sob story about being the victim of a controlling and dangerous boyfriend was disturbing, but for all I know, she could have stolen his wallet and done a runner.

"Thanks for not turning your back on me," Gianna says. She glances hesitantly at Adele as if sensing she isn't warming up to the situation as much as I am. Adele purses her lips and fusses with her hair. I can't fault her for being wary of appearing to establish any semblance of friendship with this gatecrashing stranger. She was leery enough about making this trip to begin with, and it didn't help that Clay fed us a slew of road trip horror stories before we set out.

"Let's figure out what we want to eat before our server comes," I suggest, breaking the awkward silence, as I reach for one of the plastic menus on the table.

After we've placed our orders, I turn to Gianna. "Just so we're clear, I'm happy to give you a ride to the police station after lunch. I don't know what you meant by saying CJ is dangerous, but if you had to escape from him, I'm assuming you want to press charges."

Gianna shifts uncomfortably in her seat, pulling at the sleeve of her shirt. "No, I can't do that. I just need to get as far away from him as possible."

"Where are you planning to go without any money?" I ask.

"To my parents' place, at least for now. They live in Tennessee, just outside Franklin."

I frown, trying to picture where Franklin is on the map in my road trip App. "Is that far from Nashville?"

Adele kicks me under the table, and I almost yelp out loud at the flagrant warning not to get dragged into this any further.

"It's only a forty-five-minute drive." Gianna hesitates. "Why? Are you heading that way or something?" She glances with cautious optimism from me to Adele and then back to me again, her eyes wide as searchlights.

I wet my lips, trying to find the right words to let her down gently. "I'm sorry, Gianna, we can't take you with us, if that's what you're getting at. I'll drop you off wherever you want in Kingman, but that's as far as it goes. Adele and I need to get to New York as soon as possible." I hesitate, not wanting to divulge too many details about our specific destination, or the purpose of our trip. "A family member of mine passed away."

"I'm sorry for your loss." Gianna waits for a moment and then takes a deep breath. "I know it's a big ask, but I promise I won't be any bother if you'd be willing to take me as far as Nashville. I can have my parents meet us somewhere—of course, they'd reimburse you for my expenses." She frowns. "Either that, or I suppose I'll have to hitchhike there."

Before I can respond, the server reappears with our food and a wad of napkins. "Enjoy, ladies!" she says, as she serves up our sandwiches, before trouncing off.

Gianna dives straight into her food, eating like she's famished—forgetting, at least for the moment, that I haven't given her an answer. After several mouthfuls, she starts up again. "The thing is, I can't go to the police. Like I said, my situation's complicated. CJ's very conniving and convincing. If you take me there, they'll probably arrest me."

"Why would they do that?" Adele asks, in a tone of thinly veiled suspicion.

Gianna shrugs. "CJ will turn everything around and blame me. He'll tell them I stole his phone."

"*Did* you steal his phone?" Adele asks accusingly.

"Adele!" I protest, elbowing her. "Give her a break."

"It depends on who you believe," Gianna goes on, sounding defeated. "CJ has two phones in his name, and he lets me use one of them. But he took it away last week to punish me. I found it while he was at work and made a few calls before putting it back under the stairs where he'd hidden it. He could easily get rid of it and tell the cops I stole it. The call log would prove I was the last one to use it. That's the kind of thing CJ does. He's clever—he always manages to cover his tracks with plausible explanations."

"Why on earth do you put up with that kind of behavior?" I ask.

Gianna wipes her lips on her napkin before dropping it on her plate. "He's not always like that. Sometimes he cries and tells me he can't live without me." She hesitates. "It's ... not like he ever hits me, or anything."

"Or anything?" Adele echoes. "He's clearly verbally and emotionally abusive. Can't you see that?"

Tears glisten in Gianna's eyes. She stares morosely at the crumpled napkin on her plate. "That's why I ran. I couldn't take it anymore. He hasn't let me have my wallet, or ID, or phone, in over a week, and then, out of the blue, he insisted on driving out to the desert today. That's where we were heading after we gassed up. I had a weird feeling about it. I was afraid he was planning to hurt me."

A sickening feeling churns in my stomach. I push my plate to one side and lean my elbows on the table, locking my gaze with hers. "You said he was dangerous. How dangerous are we talking?"

Gianna picks uneasily at a piece of crust from her sandwich. "I don't know for sure, but—"

Her voice trails off and I lower my head, forcing her to maintain eye contact. "What don't you know for sure?"

She looks up at me, a tear sliding down her cheek. "I think he killed his last girlfriend."

5

___

My mouth suddenly feels dry as tree bark. I fumble for my water and take a hasty sip. I don't know what to make of Gianna's terrifying accusation. Is she for real or just trying to wind us up? I feel as if I've landed in some alternate universe, or maybe this is a set up for a reality TV show. There could be a hidden camera documenting my reaction at this very minute. I throw a quick glance around the diner, half-expecting a producer to step forward and stick a microphone in my face. This road trip was supposed to be all about Instagrammable moments for my fashion blog, showcasing my outfits against spectacular backdrops—everything from the Grand Canyon to the Nashville lights. Instead, I find myself smack dab in the middle of a murky crime drama with the very real possibility that a killer might be hunting our passenger.

"That's a very serious accusation," I say. "What makes you think he killed her?"

Gianna sucks on her bottom lip for a moment. She darts an uncertain glance at a passing server before lowering her voice. "She went missing a year ago and she's never been found. Not that the cops are looking. CJ told everyone she ran off with some other guy, but I'm not so sure."

Adele and I exchange searching looks. It sounds like speculation on Gianna's part.

"Do you have any evidence?" Adele asks, digging her nails nervously into her arm.

"Hardly," Gianna huffs. "I would have gone to the police, if I had. The point is, I think CJ was planning to get rid of me too. He was dead set on us taking this stupid trip to the desert. He said it would be a romantic camping adventure— that we'd go on hikes together, sleep under the stars, that sort of thing. He even brought his metal detector along." She hesitates, her eyes flitting between Adele and me as if to make sure she has our full attention. "The thing is, I saw him put a shovel in the camper too. When I asked him about it, he told me it was to dig up anything we find, but I'm not sure I believe him. I just don't know—" Her voice trails off and I can see in her eyes that she's picturing the camping trip taking a dark turn.

I absentmindedly reach for a cold fry from my abandoned plate, trying to assess how much credit to give Gianna's narrative. Maybe she's telling the truth, and she did the right thing bolting from CJ's truck when she did, but her story keeps getting more outlandish. I don't know what to believe. I can't ignore the fact that she's a stranger who foisted herself on us. I'm happy to spring for her lunch, but I don't want to get stuck with her and her baggage. Clay's right, there are plenty of scam artists out there, and I have no way to evaluate if Gianna's one of them. The best option is to offload her as politely as possible before we leave Kingman.

"I wouldn't have trusted him either," Adele says. "Good riddance to him."

Gianna's face crumples. "He'll find me. I know he will." She buries her face in her hands with a despondent sob.

"Sssh! It's okay," I soothe, squirming awkwardly under the curious stares of the family at the next table. "Look, you're welcome to join us while we go through the Route 66 Museum. After that, we'll drop you wherever you want to go in town: a police station, a women's shelter, maybe even a church—somewhere you can trust people to help you. We're not going to leave you at the side of the road. And you shouldn't even consider hitchhiking. It's far too dangerous."

"I'm not much into museums," Gianna replies glumly. "I'll wait for you outside. Maybe you can talk about it some more—reconsider letting me ride with you as far as Nashville. I won't be any trouble. You won't even know I'm there."

I give her a tight smile in return. It's a pretty creepy comment in light of the fact that we didn't know she was back there beneath our bags for several hours. I can almost feel the heat of Adele's disapproving glare without turning my head to look at her. It's clear she wants nothing more to do with our stowaway, and she'll let me know all about it if I even suggest reconsidering.

After settling the bill, we head out to the car and drive the short distance to the Route 66 Museum located in a beautiful brick historic building.

"It was originally used to generate electrical power for the city of Kingman," Adele tells me, when we pull into the parking lot.

"How'd you get to be such a walking encyclopedia, all of a sudden?" I say, as I turn off the car.

She shrugs. "I've been reading up on all the places we've earmarked to visit."

I turn to Gianna with an apologetic grimace. "I'm not comfortable leaving you alone in the car. If you don't want to go through the museum, you can hang out in the gift shop or find a bench somewhere and wait for us." I feel bad for making it obvious I don't trust her, but I can't risk leaving her alone with our stuff. If this is some elaborate scam, then CJ—if that's even his real name—might show up while we're in the museum and take off with all our possessions.

Tickets in hand, Adele and I push through the turnstile and enter the small museum. The minute we round the corner to the first exhibit, Adele turns to me. "We can't take her with us. I'm not driving halfway across the country with a stranger sitting behind me."

"I get it," I say, in a placating tone. "I'm not entirely comfortable with it either. Let's just walk around for a bit and enjoy the exhibits while we think it over."

"What's to think over?" Adele fires back. "What would Clay say if you told him you'd picked up a hitchhiker in Barstow—a stowaway, no less?"

I throw her an alarmed look. "We're not going to tell him anything about Gianna, or her wacko boyfriend. Clay would be worried sick. I can't do that to him. He has enough on his plate between his upcoming CPA exam and his stressful job."

Adele flattens her lips. "If you have to hide this from your husband, then you already know there's something not right about it."

"Just let me think about it for a few minutes," I insist. "If Gianna's being abused, we at least need to make sure she's safe before we leave town."

We fall silent as we begin weaving our way through the exhibits highlighting the evolution of travel along the infamous US Route 66, established in 1926.

I gesture to a life-size diorama of ragged settlers camping alongside a laden wagon. "No Venti Starbucks for those poor folks," I quip. The figures are gaunt, dust bowl refugees pinning all their hopes on a better life out west as they scavenge for scraps to boil for supper over an open fire. "I vaguely remember reading about the refugees on the Mother Road in The Grapes of Wrath in Mr. Beckman's English class," I say. "Although I was probably paying more attention to the cute water polo player who sat next to me at the time."

"That was such a depressing book," Adele replies, a catch in her voice as she contemplates the display in front of us. "You can almost see the despair in their expressions. They didn't know if they were going to make it through the next day, let alone the journey."

"Makes me feel like a loser for griping about uncomfortable hotel pillows," I add.

The next section of the museum has a more hopeful vibe; filled with colorful mercantile stores, vibrant retro diners, and vintage gas pumps. Adele and I pose for several Instagram-worthy selfies, before wandering into a spacious exhibition hall packed with curious-looking early electric vehicles that look like remarkable feats of engineering to our non-mechanical brains.

"This is the last exhibit," Adele says, motioning to the exit door a few feet away. "Decision time. We need to be on the same page before we go back out there."

"Whatever we do, we can't just turn Gianna loose," I reply. "She's only nineteen, if that. We need to do something to help her."

Adele sighs. "She's not our responsibility."

"We can't just throw our hands up and drive away," I respond, holding her gaze. Maybe it's because I grew up hearing my mother describe how hard it was to make it on her own that Gianna's story is tugging at my heartstrings. I need to try to make Adele understand where I'm coming from. "You were a bleeding-heart dust bowl refugee sympathizer, a few minutes ago. We may be living in a different era, but Gianna's no different from them. She's desperate—she has no money and no phone. She won't agree to go to the police, and it's not safe for her to be out on the road alone, so our options are limited. I can't turn my back on her. Seriously, would you be able to live with yourself if we left her here and something happened to her?"

Adele tosses her head and looks away. "This isn't what I signed up for."

I nod in acknowledgement. "I realize that, but stuff happens. We just have to adapt and sacrifice a little. It's not going to put us out that much to take her to Nashville. We'll still make all the stops we were planning on and visit all the same museums."

Adele frowns. "We don't know if we can trust her. I don't feel safe with a stranger sitting behind me. She could be a psycho, for all we know."

"Fair enough," I agree. "If we bring her along, we'll lay down a few ground rules. We'll make her show us the contents of her backpack so we can be sure she doesn't have any weapons, or drugs, or anything like that with her. And we'll let her know we're going to continue with our trip exactly as we planned. We'll get to Nashville on our time, not hers."

Adele lets out a heavy sigh. "I don't like it, but I'll agree to it on one condition—she calls her parents, and they confirm her story. I want to know for sure she's legitimate and not just using us, or worse—setting us up to rob us or something."

"That's reasonable," I say with a relieved shrug. "Let's go tell her the good news."

We exit the museum through the turnstile and find Gianna sitting in an armchair in the gift store flicking through a historical picture book. I don't miss the dirty looks the cashier is shooting her as she serves a customer at the counter.

Gianna's lips twitch into a hesitant smile when she spots us. "Do you want to look around the store?" she asks.

"No," I say in a clipped tone, one eye on the cashier who's getting ready to head our way. If we don't beat a hasty retreat, she might insist we purchase the overpriced coffee table book that Gianna's been thumbing carelessly through. "We're all set."

Gianna returns the dog-eared book to a nearby display and accompanies us out to the car.

It's almost eighty degrees outside already, and I don't want to stand around baking in the heat for too long, but we have an all-important phone call to make before we leave. "Okay, here's the deal," I tell Gianna. "We'll take you to Nashville, on our terms, and in our time, but only if your story checks out. I need you to take my phone and call your parents."

"And we'll need to check your backpack," Adele adds, folding her arms in front of her like a resource officer addressing a student suspected of stashing drugs in their book bag.

"Fine. I don't have a problem with that," Gianna says, slipping her backpack from her shoulder and holding it out to Adele.

I unlock the car and watch as Adele dumps the contents unceremoniously onto the passenger seat and begins sifting through them. There's nothing of consequence that I can see; a hooded gray sweatshirt, a cherry lip balm, a half-empty plastic water bottle, a leatherette journal with a heart-shaped lock, a hairbrush, a pack of gum, and a tube of hand lotion.

Wordlessly, Adele stuffs everything back into the bag and tosses it to Gianna. The disappointment in Adele's eyes is unmistakable. It's painfully obvious she was hoping to find something that would give us an excuse to retract our offer of a ride.

I rummage in my purse for my phone and pass it to Gianna. "Put it on speaker," I instruct her. "We want to hear the conversation firsthand."

Unperturbed, Gianna takes the phone from me and taps in a number. After a few rings, I hear a husky, "Hello?"

Adele and I exchange a loaded glance as we wait for Gianna to answer. "Dad. It's me ... Gianna."

A long pause ensues, and then he asks, "Where are you?"

"Kingman, Arizona. Things didn't work out in Las Vegas. I'm coming home for a few weeks."

"Your mother's in hospital," the man responds curtly. "If you'd call once in a while, you'd know that."

"Yeah, um ... the battery on my phone's shot. I'm calling you on a friend's phone. She's driving out to the east coast and giving me a ride as far as Nashville." Her eyes meet mine and I give an uneasy twitch of my lips in response. It makes me uncomfortable to hear her taking the liberty of labeling our relationship as friendship when all I've offered to do is give her a ride. Still, she's probably trying to put her father's mind at ease by pretending she's not traveling with strangers. It's odd she didn't mention Adele. Was it an intentional oversight or a deliberate snub?

Gianna's father clears his throat. "Aren't you going to ask how your mother's doing?"

"How's she doing?" Gianna asks, conveying a heavy dose of disinterest.

"Same as usual."

"Figured as much," Gianna replies dismissively. "So, can you pick me up in Nashville when I get there, in a couple of days?" She raises a brow at me, and I shrug. With all the stops we've planned, it might take us longer than that, but I'm not about to tie us down to a particular time and day.

Gianna's father gives a disapproving grunt. "I guess I'll have to."

"I'll need to borrow some money when I get there," Gianna goes on. "Cora's loaning me some for hotels and food along the way. I'll pay you back once I get a job."

"You've been in Vegas for a year, and you haven't saved a dime?" her father fumes.

"It's expensive to live there," she huffs. "My rent was fourteen hundred dollars."

Her father mutters something unintelligible.

"Dad?" Gianna prompts.

"You're paying me back every last penny this time," he growls.

"I will, I promise," she replies. "Got to go. Cora's waiting."

She hangs up and hands the phone back to me, fixing a cold look on Adele. "Satisfied?"

Adele grimaces and climbs into the passenger seat, slamming the door with more force than necessary. She can't have missed the fact that she was left out of the conversation entirely. I groan inwardly. If they don't make an effort to get along, this is going to be a miserable stretch of the trip to Nashville.

I open the back door of the Tahoe and begin rearranging some of our stuff so I can lift up one of the back seats for Gianna. It goes without question that I put her behind me.

If anyone's going to be strangled with a shoelace en route, it should be me. I'm the one who advocated for her.

I start up the car and, immediately, *Life is a Highway* blasts through the interior.

I discreetly turn the volume down a couple of notches. The mood in the car isn't suited to our usual off-key rocking out session, especially not with a stranger on board.

"I'm sorry about your mother," I venture, glancing in the rearview mirror once we're back on the road.

Gianna shrugs. "It's nothing new. She's been in and out of the hospital for years."

"I'm sorry. Is it serious?" I ask.

"I guess. She's not getting any better."

"Cancer?" Adele asks, her natural curiosity getting the better of her intention to huff for the next leg of the trip.

Gianna lets out a snort. "I wish. She's in a psychiatric hospital."

6
_____

The hairs on the back of my neck prickle to life. I grip the steering wheel tighter, keeping my eyes forward, not wanting to face the scorching *I-told-you-she's-a-psycho* look I know for sure Adele's directing my way. To deflect attention from my state of shock, I do the only thing that occurs to me in the moment and crank up the music. Adele promptly reaches over and switches off the stereo. She twists all the way around in her seat and stares pointedly at Gianna. "What's your mother in there for?"

I hold my breath as I glance in the rearview mirror. A curious smile plays on Gianna's lips, as though she's relishing having captured Adele's curiosity. "That's a little intrusive, don't you think?" she says, in a faux innocent tone. I sense she's toying with Adele, but she doesn't realize how tenacious my best friend can be when she wants to get to the bottom of something.

"Under the circumstances, I think we have a right to know!" Adele fires back. "If your mother's a schizophrenic who hears voices telling her to swing an axe at people, I'd like to know about it."

"Hey! Adele! Take it easy!" I say, throwing her a castigating look.

"It's fine," Gianna soothes. "I get it. If you must know, my mother suffers from clinical depression and suicidal thoughts. The only person she's a threat to is herself."

I glance back at Gianna in the mirror again, trying to communicate an apology for Adele's insensitivity, but she's pulled out her journal from her backpack and buried her nose in it.

Her answer seems to have appeased Adele's suspicions, at least for now, and we settle in for the remainder of the drive to the Grand Canyon. At one point, we stop at an incredible red rock formation, and Gianna obliges us by taking Adele's and my picture posing atop a massive boulder, hands stretched toward the sky. As we stand there marooned on our twenty-foot-high sandstone island, it suddenly occurs to me that Gianna could easily jump in the Tahoe and drive off before Adele and I have time to scramble down. Thankfully, she passes the test by dutifully taking our picture from every possible angle, allowing my trust to edge up a notch to a level two on a scale of one to ten. Even Adele drops her prickly stance and compliments Gianna on the amazing photos she's taken, when we clamber back down.

Even though the tense atmosphere in the car has lifted, it doesn't escape my notice that Gianna surreptitiously checks the road behind us from time to time. Something tells me she's making sure CJ's Dodge camper truck isn't looming on the horizon. It's on the tip of my tongue to ask her if that's what she's looking for, but I'm not sure I want to hear her answer. Her ominous words are still cycling in my head. *He'll find me. I know he will.*

After a quick stop in the town of Williams to pick up a

few toiletries and items of clothing for Gianna, we turn onto Highway 64 and begin heading north toward the Grand Canyon. It's almost dusk by the time we reach our hotel at the south rim—the only accommodation we booked in advance. I enquire about an additional room, but as I suspected, they're completely sold out so Gianna will have to bunk with us. I have a nagging feeling I'll be sleeping fitfully tonight, but it can't be helped. It's not as though I can ask her to camp in the Tahoe overnight.

"Breakfast is included, six to nine in the lounge area," the concierge chirps, as she checks us in on her touchscreen. "How many keys would you like?"

I hesitate for a nanosecond.

"Just two, please," Adele pipes up.

I nod in agreement, avoiding meeting Gianna's eyes. We're treating her like a child, but it's better to be cautious. This way, we can monitor her comings and goings. Truth be told, I feel a bit like a US Marshall escorting a prisoner across state lines. Our cross-country road trip is turning out to have more layers of potential danger to it than I could ever have anticipated.

We drop our bags and pillows in the room, and head down to the ground floor pool and hot tub. Gianna says she doesn't want to swim, but we didn't give her the option of staying in the room alone with our belongings. She agreed to our terms when we laid them out in Kingman, and to her credit, she doesn't argue the point.

I dive into the pool and begin powering back-and-forth beneath the surface of the water, relishing the ability to stretch my limbs out to their fullest after being hunched over a steering wheel for the better part of the day. Clay always tells me I'm too tense when I drive. Today, I had every reason to be. I can't help feeling guilty about hiding what I've done from him. After all the warnings he gave me, and the promises I made him, he would be livid if he knew I'd allowed a stranger in my car and hotel room. I should call him before we go to dinner, but I'm going to take the easy way out and text him instead. He'd know from my voice that something wasn't right.

The silence beneath the water is a welcome release after the pulsing of the car stereo for hours on end. I'm already tiring of our playlist, and it's only day one. Maybe I'll download an audiobook for tomorrow. Adele and I love audiobooks, but I've no idea if Gianna would be up for it. Not that it matters, she'll go along with anything we propose—she has no choice. I don't know if I've made the right decision agreeing to take her as far as Nashville, but I do know I would be racked with guilt right about now if I had left her behind in Kingman, so that's some consolation.

After completing thirty laps, I take a break at the opposite end of the tiny pool from Gianna, who's stretched out in a white plastic chaise talking to a couple of kids splashing around in the shallow end. Adele swims up to me and rests her elbows on the pool deck, breathing hard. "You realize we're going to have to take shifts sleeping tonight," she says. "One of us needs to keep an eye on her. She might take off with some of our stuff, or worse."

I lower my voice, fearful Gianna might overhear us. "You're being dramatic. I really think she's harmless. Between her crazy mother and her controlling boyfriend, she's had a rough deal."

"She's sly," Adele retorts, squeezing the water from her hair. "She came across all meek and demure when she was telling us about her abusive boyfriend, but the minute we were underway, her demeanor changed. Half the time, she acts like I'm not there, and the rest of the time she puts me down. She's trying to drive a wedge between us."

"You two got off to a bad start, that's all," I say. "She senses you don't trust her and she's responding in kind. You just need to call a truce and chill." I glance up at the oversized clock on the wall. "Ready to get out of here? Maybe we can find some common ground over dinner—try to get to know her a little better."

Adele pulls a face. "I suppose we can't even have a drink because she's underage."

"*We* can do whatever we want." I arch a brow at her. "I'm buying—so she gets lemonade."

I AGREE to take the second shift that night but, at some point, the margarita I consumed at dinner wins out and I fall into a choppy sleep. To my immense relief, I wake the following morning to the sound of gentle snores, and not the blood-splattered crime scene of my nightmares. I immediately elevate Gianna to a probationary level three on my trust barometer.

After a lackluster breakfast of rubbery eggs, paper-thin bacon, and packaged pastries, we load up the Tahoe and set out along the Grand Canyon Desert View Drive to take in the sights.

"This place is spectacular—even better than the reviews," Adele raves.

I nod, rendered speechless as I take in the scale of the jaw-dropping vistas that go on and on, each bend in the road revealing a more breathtaking rock formation than the one before. I pull over at one of the overlooks and all three of us climb out, captivated by the panoramic views of the Colorado River down below.

"Words don't do it justice," I say in a reverential tone. "I kind of wish we'd scheduled some extra time to hike around for a bit. These rock formations are like paintings."

"Yeah, there's something majestic about this place," Adele says, panning her iPhone around the backdrop of the canyon.

I glance over my shoulder to see Gianna hanging back behind a slew of tourists angling for a shot. I feel bad when I remember that she doesn't have a phone. I'm sure her parents would love to see some photos when she gets to Nashville. "Gianna! Come here!" I call to her, motioning with my hand for her to stand by the viewing railing. "I'll take your picture with the canyon backdrop."

After a minute or two of cajoling, she reluctantly steps in front of the railing. "Perfect!" I say. "I'll airdrop it to your dad's phone once we get to Nashville."

She shrugs indifferently. "Yeah, sure."

"Don't you want to show him the Grand Canyon?" I ask as I exit out of my phone App. "Or have you guys been here before?"

"Never."

"So, what do you think of it?" I prod.

She lifts her eyes and solemnly pans the horizon. "CJ told me they have Gila monsters here."

"What in the world's a Gila monster?" Adele asks in a skeptical tone.

Gianna turns and stares straight at her. "One of only two venomous lizards in the world. They use their forked tongues to detect their prey." She curls her hands into fists at her sides. "CJ enjoyed frightening me with macabre facts."

"Apparently!" Adele retorts. "Just as well you didn't take that camping trip. He might have slipped one of those creatures into your sleeping bag."

Gianna stares out at the horizon. "It would have been the perfect crime. The desert's a great place to hide a body."

Without another word, she turns and walks back to the Tahoe.

Adele and I stare at each other, slack jawed.

"That was morbid!" Adele says in a hushed voice.

I grimace as I tuck my phone into the back pocket of my denim shorts. "It's probably hitting her now that if she hadn't got out of CJ's truck when she did, she might be lying in a shallow grave someplace."

We tromp back over to the car and climb in, subdued at the heavy thought.

"Are you all right?" I ask Gianna as I start the engine.

A line of worry cuts across her forehead. "I'm trying to hold it together. It's frightening to think what might have been."

"Is that why you keep looking out the rear window?" I ask, softening my tone as I turn the car around to head back in the direction of Highway 64.

Gianna gives a jerky nod, her dark mane of hair flopping over her face, hiding her expression. "I thought I saw his camper earlier. I can't shake the feeling that he'll find me, sooner or later."

"He has no idea you're with us," I assure her.

"What if he reported me missing?" Gianna asks. "If the police check the cameras at the gas station, they'll know which vehicle I'm in."

"*Obviously*, he didn't," Adele chimes in. "Or we'd have been pulled over by now. Don't worry, the police aren't after you, and CJ's not going to find you."

Gianna twists a strand of dark hair, considering her words. "Let's hope you're right, for all our sakes."

"Okay, enough of that depressing topic," I say. "Next stop,

Flagstaff for lunch. If we had more time, I'd suggest driving the whole twenty-five miles of the Desert View Drive, but I want to make it as far as Albuquerque before nightfall."

In downtown Flagstaff, we stumble on a first-rate cafe for lunch. Over a curry roasted broccoli and cauliflower salad for me, a turkey breast and cranberry brie sandwich for Adele, and a flaky mushroom, asparagus, and caramelized onion quiche for Gianna, we start to relax and even exchange a few anecdotes from high school. Gianna proves to be an excellent storyteller when she lets loose, which is, on the one hand, highly entertaining, and, on the other, slightly disconcerting. Nothing she has said or done so far contradicts her story, but there's something duplicitous about her expression at times that I can't quite put my finger on.

Before long, we're back on the road headed for Albuquerque, New Mexico. I count at least three more occasions when Gianna turns all the way around in her seat and stares out through the rear window, but I don't see any sign of the Dodge camper truck. Seemingly, neither does she, because after a while, she dozes off in the back seat. I'm not sure if she's in a deep sleep or not, so I'm careful not to talk about her with Adele in case she's eavesdropping. When we stop at Gallup to gas up, she gets out and disappears in search of a bathroom.

Adele climbs out to stretch her legs while I pump gas. "This place looks kind of sketchy," she says, eying the drugstore across the street where three police cruisers with flashing lights are parked near the entry door.

"I wouldn't want to be here after dark," I agree. "The sooner we get back on the road, the better."

My heart begins to beat a little faster when I finish gassing up and realize Gianna hasn't returned from the restroom. I replace the nozzle in the pump and pull over into a parking spot to wait for her. "Is it just me, or is this a déjà vu kind of moment?"

Adele gives a grim nod. "I was thinking the same thing. Do you think she's done a runner on us?"

My mind goes back to the elderly man who collapsed at the gas pump in Barstow, and all the commotion around the incident. I try to envision what must have been running through Gianna's head when she took a chance and hid in the back of our car. Was she really fleeing her abusive boyfriend? Or should we be afraid of her? I shiver when I remember the shock of my fingers tangling with her hair.

I hope I don't live to regret my decision to take her to Nashville.

7

W hen Gianna walks back into view, I'm filled with equal measures of relief and disappointment. Even though I stand behind my decision, I admit I'm conflicted about bringing her along.

"About time you showed back up," Adele says. "We were beginning to think you ditched us or something."

Gianna shrugs. "I had to wait. There was only one restroom open. The others were all out of order." She gives Adele a blistering look. "It's nice to know you were worried about me. I was picturing what I'd do if you'd changed your minds and driven off without me."

Adele rolls her eyes and busies herself scrolling through her phone.

"Who's up for listening to an audiobook?" I ask, in a heightened tone of cheeriness, as I pull out of the gas station. I'm determined not to let the atmosphere in the car deteriorate to arctic conditions again. I thought Adele and Gianna had finally reached a truce of sorts after our cordial lunch in Flagstaff, but it seems they can't resist provoking one another.

"Sounds riveting," Gianna says disinterestedly.

She casts a furtive glance over her shoulder in the direction of the restrooms tucked behind the gas station, before sliding down in her seat and pulling out her journal and pen. I switch on the ignition, a feeling of unease stirring in the pit of my stomach. What was she looking at? In retrospect, it seems odd that all the restrooms but one was out of order at a busy gas station like this. Gianna was gone for almost fifteen minutes. What was she really doing back there?

Adele leans over and turns on the stereo.

"What are we listening to?" I ask.

"*Big Little Lies,* by Leanne Moriarty," she replies. "You said you wanted an audiobook. It's supposed to be really good. It was an HBO series with Reese Witherspoon, and a bunch of other big names. I can't remember who else."

Once we're underway, Adele soon loses herself in the audiobook as the narrator's Australian accent fills the car, but I find myself distracted, speculating about our passenger in the back seat and what she's writing in her journal. She scribbles in it for a bit before closing her eyes and leaning her head against the window, clutching her locked journal protectively to her chest. I have a sneaking suspicion it's full of secrets—an indictment against her abusive boyfriend, perhaps?

As we drive, I'm only half-listening to the audiobook while I read the signs for the numerous Native American trading outposts along the route. I'm tempted to stop at one of them, but we're making good time, and Gianna's sleeping, which makes things peaceful. Adele and I could easily lose ourselves in a lengthy shopping expedition. Besides, it's not like I have any real use for a woven basket or a Navajo rug. The decor in our apartment has more of a modern vibe, and

I'm planning on a neutral, modern-farmhouse color scheme for our new home.

Adele glances over her shoulder at Gianna. "That girl sure sleeps a lot." She hesitates and then sucks in a hard breath before twisting fully around in her seat. "Cora!" she hisses. "Do you see that camper truck behind us?"

My senses shoot to high alert, my heart pounding out an erratic beat. I peer anxiously in the rearview mirror looking for any sign of the filthy Dodge truck that CJ drives, but I can't see anything behind the Freightliner semitrailers blocking my view.

"Where is it?" I throw a harried glance at Adele. "I don't see it."

"It's between the semi trucks," she says in a half-whisper.

I twist my head to peer at Gianna. She's sprawled out on the seat, lips parted in sleep, oblivious to the drama that's unfolding.

"Do you see it, yet?" Adele whispers urgently.

I glance in the rearview mirror again and finally catch a glimpse of a camper truck weaving and bobbing between lanes. "Are you talking about the gray truck with the white camper shell?"

"Yes," she confirms, her voice thready.

"Are you sure that's CJ's?" I ask. "Wasn't the truck in Barstow white?"

Adele frowns. "I thought it was gray, but it was so dirty it was hard to tell. It looks like he's washed it since. Do you remember if it was an Adventurer?"

I chew on my lip, frantically racking my brain to remember the make. "I don't know. I never pay attention to that kind of thing."

"What if he's been following us this whole time?" Adele mutters.

"How's that possible?" I grip the steering wheel tighter as a thought occurs to me. Could that have been why Gianna took so long in the restroom while I was gassing up? Did she meet up with CJ? All my doubts about her come rushing back with a vengeance. Are they planning to rip us off? I breathe slowly in and out, my thoughts flapping around inside my head. I need to stay calm so Adele doesn't freak out. I'm probably jumping to wild conclusions thinking the worst of Gianna. She seems genuinely scared of CJ—it's unlikely she's faking her tears while secretly plotting something nefarious with him. "Look, we don't even know if it's CJ," I say quietly. "I'm pretty sure his truck's white."

"I remember seeing that camper at the Grand Canyon," Adele says, pulling at her hair in an agitated fashion. "We drove past it on the Desert View Drive."

"So what if we did?" I reply dismissively. "The Grand Canyon gets six million visitors a year."

"But somehow that very same camper ends up only a few cars behind us," she whispers. "It can't be a coincidence. We should wake Gianna and ask her."

I shoot Adele a horrified look. "That's a really bad idea. She'll panic if she thinks CJ's found her. Let's just keep an eye on the camper for now."

Adele fidgets nervously in her seat. "She said he was dangerous. What if he has a gun?"

I open my mouth to tell her that's ridiculous, but then I have a better idea.

"Whoa! What do you think you're doing?" Adele hisses, clutching her seat when I suddenly floor the gas and begin weaving in and out of lanes. I clock over ninety miles an hour before finally settling back into the slow lane. "Better?" I ask with a triumphant smile.

Tentatively, she peers over her shoulder. "I guess," she

admits, before sinking back down in her seat. "I think you lost him."

For the next few miles, I check in the rearview mirror constantly for any sign of the camper, but it doesn't reappear on the horizon—which makes me think I was right that it wasn't CJ's truck.

Just when I'm finally engrossed in the audiobook, Adele pokes me in the ribs. "He's back," she mutters urgently. "He's caught up with us."

I glance in the mirror at Gianna. Her eyes are still closed but it's hard to tell if she's actually asleep or half-listening to the audiobook.

"There's only one way to know for sure if he's following us," I whisper. "We need to pull off somewhere. Not here in the weeds. This looks like rattlesnake country. What's the next town?"

Adele pulls out her phone and consults her maps App. "We're coming up on Grants, about six miles ahead."

I give a curt nod. "Okay, don't mention anything about the camper truck to Gianna when we stop. We'll say we're looking for a restroom."

When I turn off the highway a few minutes later, Gianna stirs in her sleep but doesn't wake.

I drive slowly past a smattering of ramshackle houses, uninviting RV Parks, and motels in various states of disrepair. I grip the steering wheel tighter, hoping against hope that CJ doesn't follow us here. It doesn't look like the type of place where anyone would come to our rescue if we needed help.

"I see a cafe up ahead," Adele says, motioning through the window. "Let's stop there and get something to drink."

When I swing into the parking lot, Gianna jerks upright

in her seat, blinking sleepily around. "Are we in Albuquerque?"

"Halfway there," I reply, reaching into the console for my wallet. "We're just stopping for a quick soda and bathroom break."

Gianna grunts and stretches her thin arms behind her head before clambering out into the oppressive heat.

Inside the dingy cafe, an overweight woman in a dirty apron and hairnet leans back against the stovetop, arms folded across her substantial chest, eying us as if we're here to commit an armed robbery—which could be a credible threat in these parts.

"Hi," I greet her. "Hot out there today." I fan my face in an exaggerated fashion, hoping to evoke a response of some kind.

The woman's stubby eyelashes flicker over her eyes—lizard-like in the cracked folds of her face—but she says nothing. Apparently, my greeting doesn't merit more than the briefest of acknowledgements. So much for customer service.

"We'd like three sodas to go, please," I say, wrinkling my nose at the heavy stench of grease in the air. "I'll take a Diet Coke."

"Sprite for me," Adele adds, before heading to the back of the cafe where a restroom sign hangs askew over a stucco archway.

"I'll have a regular Coke," Gianna adds, when I raise my brows questioningly at her.

The cranky hairnet lady unfolds her fleshy arms and shuffles wordlessly over to the soda machine. "Large or small," she calls out with her back to us.

I order three larges and tell her to keep the change, which she pockets without a word of thanks.

"Not the friendliest part of the world," I remark, as we walk back out to the car.

"At least we lost the camper," Adele mutters in my ear.

Minutes later, we're back on the I-40, bound for Albuquerque. There's no sign of a white or a gray camper truck anywhere and I slowly begin to relax as the miles go by, convinced it was a harmless tourist and not Gianna's possessive boyfriend, after all. I consider asking her what color CJ's truck is, but she would know right away that we were being followed. Thankfully, it's turned out to be a false alarm.

By the time we reach the outskirts of Albuquerque, we're hot and hungry and dying to get out of the car and stretch our legs.

"All right, find us a hotel nearby," I say to Adele.

She turns off the audiobook and starts calling around. "I keep coming up short," she complains, after her fourth attempt to secure us a hotel. "Apparently, there's a World Rural Health convention in town."

"Try and find something a little further away from the highway," I suggest.

After a couple more fruitless attempts, she finally manages to snag us two rooms at a Comfort Inn. "Take this next exit," she says, studying her phone.

"I could use a little more warning next time," I cry, slamming on the brakes and veering onto the exit ramp.

"No kidding!" Gianna yelps, as she's jerked to one side, sending her journal flying.

"Keep left," Adele says, frowning at her phone and turning the screen sideways.

I follow her directions for the next ten minutes, but we seem to be driving away from the city center and into a seedy and dimly lit industrial zone.

"Are you sure this is right?" Gianna asks, peering around my headrest.

"Shoot! I think we took the wrong exit," Adele admits, stabbing frantically at her phone.

"We?" I echo in frustration. "I followed your directions." I pull over to the side of the road and hold out my hand for her phone. "Let me see that for a minute."

Reluctantly, she hands it over and I toggle between Yelp and Apple Maps, spotting her mistake almost immediately. "You clicked on the wrong Comfort Inn. We need to start over."

After pulling up directions to the correct location, it takes me another fifteen minutes to find the place, and it's not a heartwarming sight when we pull into the rutted parking lot.

"It's a bit run down," I say dubiously, as I survey the dilapidated exterior.

"We can make it work for one night," Adele responds. "I've called around everywhere. There's nothing else available that fits our budget. We can go somewhere nice to eat to make up for it."

After gathering up our bags and pillows, we make our way inside the hotel. A short woman with sagging jowls and several missing front teeth proceeds to check us in. Her name tag is pinned sideways on the stretched-out golf shirt she's wearing, and I have to tilt my head to read it. "Thanks, Tammy," I say as I take the key cards from her and follow Adele and Gianna into an archaic-looking elevator. We jolt and shake our way up to the third floor where our adjoining rooms live up to my low expectations.

"Well, ladies," I say looking around. "I give this place a triple D rating; dark, dingy, and drab. I guess we can suffer through it for one night." I hand one of the key cards for the adjoining room to Gianna and pocket the second one, just in case I need to access her room for some reason. Technically, she's an adult, but I feel like I've taken on the role of a surrogate parent charged with escorting her safely to her family in Nashville.

"Let's shower up and find someplace to eat," I say, trying to nail a cheery tone.

"I suggest we don't take restaurant recommendations from toothless Tammy," Adele says, falling back on one of the beds.

Gianna smirks before disappearing into the adjoining room.

I let out a silent sigh of relief as the door closes behind her. Something about her unnerves me. She doesn't exhibit the downtrodden demeanor of an abused woman. I'm beginning to think she switches the tears on and off to suit her purposes. It's liberating to have separate rooms tonight so Adele and I can speak freely. I reach for a pillow and squeeze it. "Rock hard," I say, tossing it to Adele.

"And lumpy," she adds, tossing it back. "This is why we bring our own."

"What do you feel like eating?" I ask.

"Something hearty. I'd be up for a burger and fries, and a margarita. Time to let our hair down a little. My turn to drive tomorrow."

"Sounds good to me," I say. "I'm going to jump in the shower and leave you to figure out where we're going to eat."

Less than an hour later, we're seated in The Grill on the Green. Adele orders a mango margarita and I settle on a Hawaiian margarita which, according to the cocktail menu, promises to be a fruity medley designed to sweeten the senses with a creamy, dreamy twist for the tastebuds.

"Well, does it live up to the hype?" Adele laughs, after I take my first sip.

"It's delicious," I answer, licking my lips. "Sorry you can't adult with us," I say to Gianna who's nursing an iced tea.

She shrugs. "I'm just thankful you agreed to take me to Nashville. I need to get home to my parents, especially now that my mom's back in the hospital."

"Tell us about your childhood," Adele says, setting down her glass.

There's an awkward silence, for a moment or two, before Gianna answers. "There's not much to tell. I'm an only child. My mom's a certified nutcase and my dad's a tight-fisted grouch. Neither are particularly evil or good as parents go."

I fiddle with a piece of decorative pineapple on my glass as I consider her comment. It's a strange one by a dark horse. I decide not to unpack it. Tonight is about building camaraderie, not delving into Gianna's warped childhood.

"What did you do after you graduated high school?" I ask. "Did you go to college?"

"Yeah, but I dropped out after two years." She hesitates. "CJ didn't like the idea. He thinks education's a waste of money. He wanted us to open up a business together. He thought we'd make a bunch more money that way."

"And did you?" Adele prods.

Gianna twists the ends of her napkin. "Nothing ever came of it. CJ doesn't like to work hard. He'd rather take his metal detector into the desert and hunt for treasure."

She holds my gaze as her lips curve slowly into a shrewd smile. "For some reason, he was convinced he was going to strike it rich this time."

8

I spend the night twisting and turning in the scratchy hotel bed sheets, Gianna's words whirling around in my brain. Maybe I'm being paranoid, but it felt as though she was trying to communicate something at dinner with her unnerving comment. Am I reading too much into it, or does she know about the money I've come into? No matter how much I try to convince myself that it's a ridiculous thought, I'm left wondering if I've walked into a trap.

At 7:00 a.m. I stumble out of bed and into the shower, the shock of the water jolting my frayed nerves fully awake. I dry off and wrap a threadbare bath towel around myself, still fighting an uneasy feeling in the pit of my stomach. "All yours," I say to Adele, as I exit the bathroom. "Don't breathe too deeply in there. It smells of mold."

"Ugh, great! What do you want to do for breakfast?" she asks, stifling a yawn as she perches on the end of the bed. "I'm not excited about whatever fare they include here with our lumpy beds."

"Let's find a Starbucks or something," I suggest. "I need some real coffee or I'm going to fall asleep at the wheel."

"My turn to drive today, remember?" Adele stops raking her fingers through her hair and inspects me more closely. "What's the matter? You look awful. Does my driving scare you that much?"

I sink down next to her and give a chagrined shrug. "I couldn't sleep. I couldn't stop thinking about what Gianna said at dinner—that CJ thought he was going to strike it rich this time. Did you see the weird look she gave me when she said it?" A shiver trickles down my spine at the memory of her disturbing smile. "It's probably stupid, but it almost made me think she knows about my inheritance."

Adele tilts a brow. "That's impossible, but she's a strange fish—I'll give you that. I still think that was CJ in the camper truck behind us. I don't know if they've cooked up some scheme between them, or if she's really trying to get away from him, but this whole situation makes me nervous. The sooner we get to Nashville, the better."

I let out a heavy sigh. "I still think we did the right thing. We couldn't have kicked her out of the car after hearing her story—not if there's even a chance she's being abused." I get to my feet with an air of determination. "I'll knock on her door and make sure she's awake."

I dig into my suitcase and select a vibrant floral shift dress and leather sandals. After dressing, I unlock the adjoining door to Gianna's room and knock on her side. I wait for a moment or two, then jiggle the handle, before knocking again, louder this time. When there's still no response, I grab the key to her room and head out into the hallway. I rap my knuckles on her door, shuffling impatiently from one foot to the other, all the while smiling awkwardly at the other hotel guests making their way down to breakfast. After waiting for several frustrating minutes, I insert the key card into the door and push it open.

"Gianna? Are you awake?" I peer around the room taking in the unmade bed and pillows tossed onto a nearby chair. She could be in the bathroom, although I don't hear any water running. I tap lightly on the door before pushing it open. The hotel toiletries have been used and there are dirty towels lying on the floor. I take another look around the bedroom and peek inside the mirrored closet, looking for her backpack, but there's no sign of it. Maybe she's an early riser and went downstairs to get a coffee or something. She could have shown us the courtesy of letting us know, but at least this means she's not going to make us run late.

When I return to my room, Adele's still in the shower, so I decide to give Clay a quick call to make up for the generic one-line text I sent him last night after dinner.

"Hey, you!" he answers. "How's everything going?" I can tell he's trying to strike a casual note, but there's anxiety threaded through his voice. He's always been a worrywart when it comes to my ability to cope without him. In his mind, the further east I drive each day, the more the risk of something going wrong increases.

"Everything's great," I gush. "We're having a blast." I can hardly divulge that we've picked up an abused women with an unhinged boyfriend and a mother with psychiatric issues. "We're taking tons of pictures. The scenery in New Mexico is beautiful. Did you check out my Instagram, yet?"

"Yeah, the pictures look great." He hesitates and then clears his throat. "Who took that one of you and Adele on top of the huge boulder?"

I wet my lips to lubricate the lie about to slip from them. "Oh, some random family that had stopped to let their dog out."

"You need to be careful about strangers in remote locations like that," Clay chides. "You never know who you're talking to when you stop alongside the road."

"Relax, babe! It was just off the I-40. We were perfectly safe."

"People are assaulted and robbed all the time when they stop or break down," Clay responds. "You can't be so nonchalant about it."

Adele comes waltzing out of the bathroom with a towel turban-wrapped around her head, and I seize the opportunity to avoid getting into an argument with Clay.

"Gotta go," I say. "Adele and I are heading out for breakfast. I'll call you again this evening."

He mumbles a disgruntled goodbye before hanging up.

I groan and drop my iPhone into my purse.

"Clay still feeling sorry for himself?" Adele asks, a hint of amusement in her voice.

"He's hanging in there. Still giving me the stranger-danger talk, though."

Adele frowns. "Did you tell him about Gianna?"

"No! Of course not!"

"Good. Is she awake?" Adele asks, rubbing her hair vigorously.

"Yeah, she's not in her room though, and her backpack's gone. Looks like she showered up already and went downstairs. We should get going too."

Adele tosses her towel on the bed. "As much as that girl sleeps in the car, I'm not surprised she's up and out before us. I'll be ready in a jiffy."

After packing our suitcases, we make our way down to the first floor where the complimentary breakfast buffet is located in the far corner of the lobby. A line of people shuffles their way slowly around the chafing dishes, heaping their plates while balancing paper cups of coffee in one hand. Serving staff hustle around refilling the dishes and replacing the insipid-looking selection of breakfast items. I scan the crowd for Gianna, but there's no sign of her. Most of the tables are occupied or piled high with discarded dishes. A few kids are chasing each other around a pile of suitcases that appear to belong to a tour group, judging by the colorful matching tags. Adele and I merge with the fray, expecting to find Gianna tucked away at a table in the back.

"I don't see her anywhere," Adele says, craning her neck to peer through the sea of bodies.

"Maybe she grabbed some coffee and went outside," I say. "She might not have wanted to sit at a table by herself. Let's head out to the car and see if we can spot her."

After loading up our bags in the Tahoe, we scour the parking lot for any sign of Gianna, and even walk around the side of the hotel hoping to find her lounging on a bench or perched on a retaining wall sipping her coffee. At this point, I'm starting to get irritated. I made it clear this trip was going to happen on our schedule, and I don't want to have to hang around the hotel waiting on her. "I hope she didn't decide to go for a walk," I say.

Adele throws me a skeptical look. "At this time of the morning? Not likely. She can't have gone looking for a decent coffee shop either—she doesn't have any money."

"She does have a few dollars on her," I say. "I gave her cash to pay for those items she picked up at the store in Williams, and I didn't bother asking for the change—I figured she could use the money."

"Great," Adele huffs, folding her arms across her chest as she leans back against the Tahoe. "Now we're stuck at this dump waiting on her to show up whenever she feels like it."

"Let's go back inside and make sure she's not there," I suggest. "We can ask the concierge if he remembers seeing her this morning. I'll show him that picture I took of her at the Grand Canyon."

Adele gives an irritated nod. "It's really inconsiderate of her. We're doing her the favor."

Back inside the hotel, we conduct another cursory search of the lobby and buffet area before making our way over to the reception desk. I smile politely at the acne-pitted young man stationed behind the counter. "Good morning! We're looking for a friend of ours. She was staying in 206— we were in the adjoining room, 208. I was wondering if you saw her this morning." I slide my phone across the counter and swivel it around so he can see the photo of Gianna.

He frowns and pushes his glasses up his nose. "Yeah, she left already."

"When? Did we just miss her?"

The concierge blinks, a slightly confused look rippling across his brow. "She's long gone. She left a few minutes after I started my shift at 4:00 a.m."

9

"**A**re you sure she hasn't returned?" I ask the concierge as he hands me back my phone.

He casts a distracted glance over my shoulder at an elderly couple standing in line behind us. "I can't say for sure," he replies. "Would you mind stepping aside for a minute while I check these people out?"

I try to tamp down the panic mounting inside me. According to the concierge, Gianna's been gone for hours. I huddle with Adele at the end of the counter, not wanting anyone to overhear our conversation. "Where on earth could she have gone at four o'clock in the morning?" I mutter.

Adele grimaces. "It's pretty obvious, isn't it? She's dumped us. She has no intention of traveling to Nashville with us. I bet she hitched a ride back to Barstow—or maybe CJ picked her up."

"You're making a lot of assumptions," I say. "What if something's happened to her? I feel responsible. We brought her here, and she's only nineteen."

Adele flicks her wrist at me impatiently. "She's an adult. She's free to run back to her loser boyfriend if that's what she wants to do. We've wasted enough time on her already. We need to get going if we still want to look around the Old Town area before we leave."

I chew on my nail as I dart an anxious glance around the bustling lobby. "We can't just leave without her. Her parents are expecting her to show up in Nashville. I'll run back upstairs and check her room one more time. You stay here in case she turns back up."

"Whatever," Adele says in a disgruntled tone. She wanders over to a seating area next to a potted plant in a quieter part of the lobby to wait for me.

The elevator is taking forever with so many people trying to check out, so I take advantage of the fact that I'm bag free and jog up the emergency exit stairs to the third floor. As I suspected, Gianna's room is vacant. I was half-hoping she might have slipped back in undetected and fallen asleep. This is beginning to freak me out, and I have no idea how to handle the situation. Gianna may be an adult, but she was traveling in my vehicle, staying here on my ticket, and now she's disappeared under my watch. I can't just drive off without knowing she's all right. If she did decide to go back to CJ, she should at least have had the decency to tell us. I flip through the notepad next to the phone in case she left a note, but it's blank.

Back in the lobby, I make a beeline over to Adele who's slouched in a lounge chair watching the kids running circles around the lobby. When she sees me approaching, she straightens up and eyes me critically. "I'm guessing by your expression you didn't find her."

"I don't know what to do," I say glumly. "We can't abandon her without making sure she's okay."

Adele snorts. "We're not abandoning her—she abandoned us."

I rub my brow, weighing our options. "Let's go get coffee and see if she's returned by then."

With an air of reluctance, Adele gets to her feet and follows me out to the car. Thankfully, it's her turn to drive today. I'm too much of a mess inside to concentrate on navigating an unfamiliar city. Clay would be beside himself if he knew I'd relegated the task to Adele. I'll just have to hope for the best that she doesn't sideswipe somebody.

I spend the entire time scouring sidewalks for any sign of Gianna. Each time I spot a dark-haired woman with a black backpack, I perk up, and then slowly deflate when I realize it's not her.

Adele and I get our Starbucks breakfast order to go and sip our lattes in silence on the drive back to the Comfort Inn. As we're pulling into the parking lot, a large coach pulls out. We hurry back inside to find that the lobby has cleared out. I quickly scan the few remaining guests dotted around the tables in the buffet area, but to no avail. "I'm going to ask to speak to a manager," I say to Adele. "Maybe they can search the hotel grounds. It's possible Gianna wasn't feeling well and passed out in a stairwell or something."

Adele tightens her lips as if to refrain from expressing what she's really thinking. "Do what you need to do."

I make my way back over to the reception desk and ask the concierge if I can speak to a manager. The Adam's apple in his throat bobs as he sizes me up. "You're not in any trouble," I reassure him. "I just wanted to leave my contact information in case my friend shows back up."

He gives a relieved nod as he reaches for the phone behind the counter. After relaying a brief summary of the situation to someone on the other end of the line, he replaces the handset and beams at me. "The manager will be out in a few minutes to speak with you."

I thank him and move to one side so he can take care of the other guests in line. Several minutes go by before a short woman with a slick blonde bob, dressed in a crisp white shirt, emerges from the back room. The concierge points her in my direction, and she walks over to me with a confident stride and stretches out a hand. "I'm Sierra Caldwell, what can I do for you?"

After introducing myself, I give her a carefully edited rundown of the situation. I'm reluctant to tell her that Gianna stowed away in my car. It sounds too farfetched. She might think we're part of a trafficking ring. "To be honest, it's a little awkward because we don't know her all that well," I explain. "It's a long story, but she's sort of a friend of a friend, and I got talked into giving her a ride to her parents' place in Nashville. It's possible she may have changed her mind and decided to go back to her boyfriend and been too embarrassed to tell us—he's a bit of a jerk."

"Have you tried calling her?" Sierra enquires.

"Uh … she left her phone in her boyfriend's truck," I say sheepishly.

Sierra whisks out a walkie-talkie. "I'll have security do a sweep of the premises and conduct a welfare check in her room. In the meantime, we can review the security footage together and make sure it was actually your friend who left this morning. Give me a few minutes to sort things out."

I nod gratefully, relieved to leave it in her capable hands, and head back to Adele to give her an update.

"Sounds like we're going to be here for a while, after all," she says with a frustrated sigh. "I'll grab my iPad from the car so we can work out where we want to stop off today."

"Good idea," I reply. "I'll walk out with you."

I unlock the Tahoe and wait for Adele as she rummages around for her iPad. "Can you see if it's in the back anywhere?" she calls to me. "It might have fallen between the seats."

I open the rear passenger door and dig around under the driver's seat. My fingertips brush up against something hard and I pull it out, expecting to see an iPad.

It's Gianna's journal!

10

"Do you see it anywhere?" Adele calls to me, as she scrabbles around in the passenger door pocket.

"Uh, no," I say, clutching the journal to my chest. "But ... I found something else."

Adele leans around the passenger seat headrest, her eyes widening. "Is that Gianna's?"

I nod. "She won't be too happy when she realizes she's forgotten it. Makes me think we haven't seen the last of her."

"CJ's not going to let her come back for a stupid journal," Adele scoffs.

"Depends on what's in it. If it's a diary of abuse at his hands, it could be incriminating. No sign of your iPad anywhere?"

Adele shakes her head. "I know I didn't bring it into the hotel last night. I was sure it had fallen down between seats." She furrows her brow. "You don't think Gianna took it, do you?"

"No. She'd hardly risk biting the hand that feeds her."

Adele twists her lips. "Except we're not feeding her

anymore, are we? I just find it suspicious that right when my iPad goes missing, she's nowhere to be found."

"Let's not jump to conclusions, yet," I say. "Your iPad's probably buried under our mountain of stuff." I slide Gianna's journal into the pocket on the back of my seat. "It's got to be in the car somewhere. I'm guessing something got thrown on top of it."

We spend the next ten minutes tearing the car apart, but there's no trace of Adele's iPad anywhere. Although I defended Gianna's innocence, deep down I can't help wondering if she did steal the iPad. Even if she was telling the truth about running away from CJ, she never struck me as trustworthy—there was something about her that didn't add up. "Are you absolutely sure you didn't bring your iPad up to the room?" I ask Adele.

"Positive. I couldn't find it when we checked in. I remember thinking I would look for it after dinner because I wanted to charge it overnight, but that mango margarita went to my head, and I forgot all about it."

"Well, it's not in the car, that's for sure," I say, slamming the rear door of the Tahoe shut. "We should go back inside and see if they've searched the hotel yet. I'm sure the manager's wondering where we are."

We make our way over to the reception desk, and Sierra wastes no time conducting us into her office. "Let's start by confirming that it was your friend who left this morning. I'd like you to look at the security footage from the lobby area," she says, turning her computer screen toward us. I lean forward, scarcely daring to breathe, my eyes riveted on the grainy black-and-white film. At exactly 4:11 a.m., a long-haired, female figure exits through the front door, fingers hooked through the straps of her backpack. There's no mistaking the familiar profile. "That's Gianna," I say.

"Yeah, it's definitely her," Adele agrees.

Sierra nods and turns her screen back around. "I've checked the remainder of the footage from this morning, and I can confirm that she hasn't returned to the hotel since. My security personnel have conducted a sweep of the premises and also a welfare check in her room. I'm afraid it looks as if your friend left without you."

"Acquaintance," Adele corrects her.

I throw Adele a reproving look. Does she really need to make a point of conveying her dislike of Gianna at a time like this? "We appreciate everything you're doing to help, Sierra," I say, in a bid to compensate for Adele's tart tone. "We're going to take a look around Albuquerque's Old Town area for an hour or two, and then we'll check back with you on the off-chance Gianna's returned by then. She might have gone for a walk and got lost or something. Like I mentioned earlier, she doesn't have her phone with her."

Sierra interlaces her fingers on the desk. "If you want to report your friend missing—" She catches herself mid-sentence and shoots Adele a chagrined look. "If you decide to report your acquaintance as a missing person, I'd be happy to turn over our security footage to the authorities."

"Thank you," I say, getting to my feet. "We'll stop back by in a couple of hours and make a decision then. Maybe we can extend our checkout time until noon, just in case?"

"Certainly. I'll let housekeeping know. Take your time," Sierra assures us.

Adele and I make our way out to the Tahoe and climb in. She turns to me as I'm buckling up. "Want to take a peek at Gianna's journal?"

My stomach twists. I'd momentarily forgotten all about it. "We'd have to break the lock. That's an invasion of her privacy. What if she comes back for it?"

Adele narrows her eyes. "What if there's something important in it?"

I turn to look out the window, weighing her words. The journal might contain a clue to Gianna's whereabouts—a phone number or an address. If nothing else, it's proof that she was in our car. It will be a key piece of evidence in the event we report her missing. "Let's wait and see if she shows back up at the hotel in the next couple of hours. If not, we'll turn the journal over to the police."

Adele lets out a frustrated breath as she starts up the car and backs out of our parking spot. "I don't see why we have to involve the police. I don't want to get dragged into her mess any more than we already are. If she's moved on from us, then she's on her own, as far as I'm concerned."

"Don't you want to report the theft of your iPad?" I ask.

"What good would it do? We don't know where she lives. We don't even know her last name."

I blow out a breath. "True. Okay, let's just forget about Gianna for the next hour or two and enjoy some sightseeing. We'll figure out what to do if she's not back by the time we're done." I pull out my phone and Google Old Town Albuquerque. "Hmm ... it says here it was established by a group of Spanish families in 1706. It has retained its charming character with adobe architecture, and it's chock-full of history, museums, shopping, and culture." I turn to Adele and grin. "Sounds right up our alley."

"I'm in, especially the shopping part!" Adele says.

"Ditto," I agree, scrolling through the list of stores. "This emporium I'm looking at sells gorgeous turquoise jewelry. We're definitely going there."

"Okay, directions to the public parking lot, please," Adele says.

Old Town more than lives up to its reputation, and

Adele and I end up taking a bunch of selfies for my fashion blog in front of its delightful succulent gardens, terracotta urns, fountains, and picturesque store fronts. The rest of the morning we spend browsing in gift stores packed to the hilt with handmade art and crafts. Adele purchases a couple of colorful woven blankets and I select a set of decorative tile coasters. Clay will turn up his nose at them—he prefers everything sleek and modern—but I want to have a few souvenirs of our trip.

By the time we arrive back at the Comfort Inn, it's almost noon. I thought about just calling Sierra, but I want to take one last look around Gianna's room in case I missed something. Adele pulls into a parking spot close to the front door and leaves the engine running. "I'll wait here. There's no sense in us wasting any more time if she hasn't shown back up."

"We still need to go to the police station and file a missing person's report before we get back on the road," I remind her.

Adele purses her lips. "We should wait on that. The police won't do anything, anyway. Gianna's an adult and she hasn't been missing for twenty-four hours, yet. I bet she calls or texts at some point today when she's put enough distance between us. She might want us to mail that journal to her."

I throw her a skeptical look. "She'll hardly contact us again if she stole your iPad."

"That won't faze her. She'll simply deny knowing anything about it." Adele fires me an indignant look. "And you can forget about getting your money back for hotel rooms and meals. Her father won't be compensating you for anything if you show up in Nashville without his daughter."

I climb out of the car, still hoping Gianna's disappearance will turn out to be a misunderstanding. I don't feel good about the turn things have taken. My conscience craves some reassurance that she's okay.

But my gut's telling me she isn't.

S tomach churning, I make my way inside the Comfort Inn to the reception desk. As I suspected, Sierra confirms that Gianna still hasn't returned. After checking both of our rooms one last time, I turn in the keys and make my way out to the Tahoe feeling dejected, and more than a little fearful. I can't shake the thought that something has happened to Gianna. Did CJ find her? Based on everything she told us, I can't imagine she would have gone with him willingly. As I approach the car, I notice Adele talking on the phone, looking distraught as she flails her arms around. She startles when I open the door. "Gotta run. Talk later," she mutters into the phone. She drops it into her purse and turns to me. "Any news?"

"Negative," I reply, yanking on my seatbelt. "Who were you talking to? You looked upset."

A weary expression settles on her face. "My mom. Jackson's acting up again. As usual, my parents want me to sort things out."

"I'm sorry," I say, giving her an awkward smile. I can't help feeling guilty that she's stuck trying to manage the situation from afar. Her parents are older, and not in the best of health, and she's the only one who can get through to her knucklehead brother. "Do you want me to drive so you can talk to him?"

"No, it's all right, I'll call him later when he's had time to simmer down. Ready to get out of here?" Adele asks, switching on the ignition.

I give a hesitant nod. "There's nothing more we can do about Gianna for now. Maybe you're right and she'll touch base with us at some point. In the meantime, we might as well get on with making the most of our adventure."

"Where are we off to now?" Adele asks.

"Next stop, Cadillac Ranch for an Instagrammable extravaganza," I announce with a flourish.

"We still have that spray paint we picked up at Walmart, right?" Adele asks.

"Yeah, I saw it back there when I was looking for your iPad."

"I'm psyching myself up to add my lame artistic contribution to the graffiti fest." Adele chuckles. "I mean, what else are you supposed to do at a roadside attraction of Cadillacs buried nose down in the dirt?"

"We can't sing and we can't paint. What good are we?" I say, dissolving into laughter. The mood in the car lightens, and before long, we're belting our way through *Mustang Sally*, and bopping to the music in our seats. It's liberating not having a stranger sitting behind us listening in on our conversation. We're having such a rip-roaring good time that we almost miss the exit to Cadillac Ranch. "That's us!" I blurt out, wagging my finger at the sign up ahead. "Exit sixty!"

Adele slams on the brakes and takes a hard right to catch the offramp just in the nick of time. I brace myself so I don't go sliding across the seat. A horn behind us blares, and I catch a glimpse of someone shaking a fist at us through the window. Clay would have a fit if he'd witnessed Adele's reckless maneuver.

"Thanks a bunch! Some navigator you are," she sputters, as we slow to a halt at the infamous Cadillac Ranch.

We park along the shoulder and dig out our spray cans. Neither of us has much artistic ability, but we're determined to leave our mark and take some pictures to show our grandkids one day. Adele takes dibs on the first Cadillac and shoos me over to the neighboring one. I search in vain for an open area on one of the panels. Some of the people who've visited are exceptionally talented—it seems a shame to cover up their handiwork. I pick a spot that doesn't look particularly pretty to begin with and shake up my can. "Here goes nothing!" I call to Adele.

I've just stepped back to evaluate my efforts when my phone rings. My mind immediately goes to Gianna. I fumble in my pocket, my hopes dashed when I see Clay's name on the screen. "Hey babe," I say breathlessly. "What's up?"

"You sound like you've been running," he responds.

"Not running—painting. We're at Cadillac Ranch. Check us out on Instagram later."

"I will. Everything going okay, still?"

I force myself to smile so it doesn't sound as if I'm trying to hide anything. It's been a rough morning so far, but I'm definitely not going to bring up the drama with Gianna. Or Adele's near miss on the highway getting here. "Absolutely! We're having a blast. Although, Jackson's been acting up again, so that's a bit worrisome. Adele was on the phone with her mom earlier. I could tell she was upset about it."

"What do you mean she was upset? What did she say?" Clay asks, sounding worried.

"Not much. It's a stressful situation. Her parents can't cope with him. She's the only one who can ever rein him in, and he knows she can't do much when she's this far away, so I think he's making the most of it."

"Well, their parents are just going to have to step up and deal with him now, aren't they?" Clay replies, a sarcastic edge to his tone.

"There's no need to be such a chump about it," I reply, my voice rising to a defensive level. "She's concerned for her parents. They're not in good health."

"I told you it wasn't a good idea for her to go with you on this trip," Clay says. "What if something happens and she has to fly home?"

I scratch my brow. "You mean to her brother, or her parents?"

"Either one! What difference does it make? Why are you being so evasive?"

I shake my head in disbelief. "I don't know what you're talking about. I'm standing in the middle of a field with a can of spray paint in my hand. And you're mad at me because I told you Adele's upset about her brother. Seriously? Maybe you could offer to help instead of scoffing at her parents. How about you go over there and try talking some sense into Jackson?"

"Now, you're being dramatic. Maybe you should get out of the sun. I'll call you later when you've cooled off," Clay snaps, before hanging up.

I slide my phone into my pocket, shaking with rage. What is he so worked up about—accusing me of being evasive, and dramatic? Does he sense I'm hiding something from him? I've left him completely in the dark about the situation with Gianna, which could become a wedge between us if it comes to light later on. And the way things are going, it might. The truth is, I'm going to have to decide whether or not to report her missing if we don't hear from her by tomorrow. I can't show up in Nashville without her—not with her father waiting for a call to pick her up.

"Picture time," Adele chirps, walking up to me and slinging an arm casually over my shoulder. "Smile for the paparazzi!" She grins and snaps a selfie of us standing in front of my feeble attempt at modern art.

I flash a frozen smile for the camera, still shaking inwardly at my verbal confrontation with Clay.

"Ugh!" Adele says, studying the picture on her phone. "You look like you're sucking on a lemon."

I grimace. "I just got into it with Clay. I think he knows I'm keeping something from him. But it's not like I can tell him about Gianna. He'll go ballistic."

Adele links her arm in mine as we trudge back through the field to the Tahoe. "Shake it off. We'll go out for a bang-up Texas-style BBQ tonight and celebrate with a glass of wine, now that we don't have to babysit our creepy passenger anymore."

Despite Adele's best efforts to cheer me up, my mood has been dampened by the argument with Clay. The magnitude of what I'm hiding from him is beginning to sink in. Once he finds out that I agreed to drive a stowaway with a dangerous boyfriend to Nashville—a boyfriend who may have killed a woman—he's going to blow his top. I don't like keeping things from him, but I don't want him distracted and worrying about me either with his CPA exam looming on the horizon.

We settle back into the drive and soon find ourselves walled in on both sides of the I-40 by massive wind farms. It's a fascinating sight, but also somewhat disturbing—a steel invasion that has eaten up every inch of wildlife habitat for mile after endless mile. I dread to think what happens to any unsuspecting birds that collide with the fast-spinning blades.

"I can't believe the size of those turbines," Adele observes. "And there are so many of them. We've been driving for miles and all I can see on either side of the highway is a sci-fi forest of steel."

"I had no idea Texas produced so much wind power," I reply. "I thought it was the oil state."

"They certainly have the conditions for wind power," Adele says. "All these gusts of wind are making it feel as though the Tahoe could flip at any minute."

I shoot her a nervous glance. "Keep both hands on the wheel. Do you want me to drive?"

"Relax! I've got it," Adele replies, training her eyes on the road ahead.

"In that case, I'm going to start looking for a hotel," I say. "We can spend the night in Texas and then hit the next stop on our list tomorrow—the National Memorial and Museum in Oklahoma City."

Adele wrinkles her brow. "Remind me what that is again."

"It's to commemorate the Oklahoma City bombing," I say. "My neighbor told me to check it out. Her aunt worked in the Federal building, and she was badly injured in the blast—she walked with a limp for the rest of her life. A bunch of people died." I reach for my phone and Google it. "One-hundred-and-sixty-eight people in all, nineteen of them were kids."

Adele shivers. "That's horrific. Was it terrorists?"

I glance over the information on the website. "No. It was a disgruntled American ex-soldier who hated the govern-ment—Timothy McVeigh."

"Did they ever catch him?"

"Yeah, they arrested him the same day. It says here he was executed by lethal injection on June 11, 2001."

"At least they got him. Not that it brings anyone back." Adele rolls her shoulders. "It's hot. I'm ready to get out of this car. How are you doing on that hotel?"

"There's a Holiday Inn Express about ten miles down the road in the town of Shamrock," I say, turning off the music. "I'll call and see if I can get us a room."

Fifteen minutes later, we pull into the hotel parking lot. I retrieve our cases from the back of the car and hesitate, looking at Gianna's empty seat. Her journal is right there where I left it, sticking out of the pocket. Adele's right. There might be something important in it—perhaps even a message asking for help.

My mind made up, I walk around to the rear door and reach for the journal. It's time to find out what was going on in our mysterious stowaway's head.

12

The minute we step into our room, Adele tosses her purse on a chair and eyes the journal impatiently. "Go on, then. What are you waiting for?"

I give an uneasy shrug. "I feel bad about violating Gianna's privacy. Then again, I suppose I'd feel worse if it turned out she'd left us a message asking for help, or a clue to where she went and why. I just want to rule out the possibility that she's in danger."

"Quit trying to talk yourself into it. Just do it!" Adele says, flopping down on one of the queen beds. "Technically she broke into the Tahoe, so this makes us even."

I slip off my denim jacket and pull the journal from my shoulder bag. With a reverent air, I run a hand over the geometric cover as if I'm handling a sacred book.

"Hurry up!" Adele urges.

"I'll need a bobby pin or something," I say, rummaging around in my purse. I remove the metal paperclip from a sheaf of printouts on places we're planning to visit and start jiggling it in the tiny lock on the journal. After three tries, I hear the satisfying click of the lock springing open.

I take a deep breath as I flip open the book. Adele pats a spot on the bed, and I sink down next to her. She leans in closer as I begin to turn the pages. Most of them are filled with random sketches or motivational words and phrases in intricate shaded lettering; *Believe, There is always light, Keep on dreaming.* "She's a skilled artist," I say admiringly. "She could have really dressed up those Cadillacs we disfigured."

"She's definitely got the magic touch," Adele agrees grudgingly.

I continue turning pages, riveted by the meticulous details in even the smallest of the sketches. Some are deeply moving—intensely personal self-portraits: Gianna holding a hand in front of her face as if to protect herself, leaning against a wall with a solitary tear trickling down her cheek, staring out the window with a hollow look in her eyes—self-portraits of an abused woman. I can't help squirming, knowing these evocative images weren't intended for strangers' eyes. I exchange a guilty look with Adele, emboldened by the fact that she doesn't appear to be in the least bit rattled by what we're doing.

I turn a few more pages, and then my fingers turn to ice. Adele tenses next to me, her nails digging into my arm as we stare at a charcoal sketch of ourselves. It's drawn from Gianna's vantage point in the rear seat, so all we can really see is the back of our heads and a grisly side profile of Adele's face cut away to depict the bone and sinew beneath. My skin crawls at the thought of Gianna unobtrusively sketching us while we drive. I'm so busy staring at the freakish picture that, at first, I don't even notice what's written next to it. It's only the grim expression on Adele's face that makes me take a closer look.

One of us won't survive this road trip. Kill or be killed.

I gasp in horror, the journal almost slipping from my

hands. "What's that supposed to mean? Is she talking about us, or herself?"

"I ... I don't know, but whatever she had in mind, it's giving me the creeps," Adele answers.

I frantically skim through the remaining pages in the journal. The sketch of our heads was the last entry, which makes it seem all the more ominous. I can't decipher its meaning. Did Gianna have murder in mind, or was she predicting her own death at CJ's hands? *He'll find me. I know he will.*

Adele narrows her eyes. "She might have deliberately left her stupid journal behind to freak us out. This is all just a game to her. You've seen how her whole demeanor changes in a heartbeat. One minute she's in tears, and the next she's grinning at us like the Joker. I'm guessing CJ was behind us the entire time. They were planning something. Maybe they decided it was too risky to rob us, so she pinched my iPad and took off."

I stare at Adele, weighing her words with a growing sense of unease. "What if they're still following us? I shouldn't have told her I had a relative who passed away. She might have guessed I'd been left some money. Maybe she thinks she can get her hands on it somehow." I chew on my lip, deeply regretting not kicking Gianna to the curb when I first discovered her hiding in the Tahoe. I should have known it wouldn't end well. I can already hear Clay's voice berating me. *What were you thinking? Don't you listen to anything I say? I told you something like this would happen!*

I slam the journal shut. "We have to take this to the police first thing in the morning. Whether something's happened to her, or she's in cahoots with CJ, I won't be able to rest easy until we locate her."

Adele snatches the journal out of my hand, her face

paling. "Are you out of your mind?" She lowers her voice, as though Gianna were still in the room with us. "We can't show this to the police. They could interpret it to mean we did something to Gianna. *One of us won't survive this road trip* —she was sketching us when she wrote that, and now she's disappeared. We were the last ones to see her. There's a good chance the police will suspect we had something to do with her disappearance."

My stomach roils when I recognize the truth of what she's saying. As I stare at the journal, my breathing grows more labored, the weight of the words sitting like a bear on my lungs. This whole situation has gone from bad to worse overnight. No matter what move I make, it could be a fatal mistake. If Gianna has fallen victim to a crime—likely at CJ's hands—then I owe it to her to turn her journal over to the police and report her as missing. On the other hand, if she and CJ have set up some elaborate plot to prey on us, the last thing I want to do is end up a suspect in her disappearance. I plunge my hands through my hair, trying to unravel my scrambled thoughts. My mind is spiraling into a pit of despair, picturing one horrific scenario after another. Gianna's parents are expecting us to show up in Nashville with her any day now—she used my phone to call them which means they have my phone number. If we can't explain her disappearance, and we can't locate her, Adele and I will be under a cloud of suspicion. "I don't know what to do," I say, dropping my face into my hands.

"Nothing," Adele says firmly. "We did nothing wrong, and we're not involved in whatever scheme Gianna and her loser boyfriend cooked up between them. We're going to forget all about her and pretend we never met her."

I cast a doubtful look at Adele. "What about her journal?"

Adele hesitates, rubbing her thumb back and forth over the cover. "We'll have to get rid of it."

I pick at the skin on my finger, uncomfortable with the finality of it. Destroying the journal means admitting that something nefarious has happened. I'm still holding out for a simple explanation that will make this whole nightmare implode. "Let's hang on to it, for now," I say, retrieving it from Adele's lap. "If Gianna doesn't contact us, we'll ditch it once we reach Katonah."

I WAKE the following morning to the sound of an unfamiliar beeping. For a moment or two, I lay perfectly still in bed with my eyes closed, trying to figure out if I'm dreaming.

Adele groans and throws back her duvet. "Do you hear that? The battery in the fire sprinkler's dead."

I roll over and stretch before sitting up in bed. "What time is it?"

"Almost five-thirty. We might as well get up and get on the road now that we're awake."

I slide my feet to the floor and trudge over to the window. It looks like it's going to be a beautiful day, not a breath of wind in sight. I quickly scan the cars in the parking lot until my eyes land on the Tahoe. It's always reassuring to confirm that it hasn't been broken into overnight and all our stuff stolen. My gaze drifts sleepily to the far end of the parking lot. I frown, rubbing my eyes to clear my vision. My fingers fumble with the drapery pull rod as I yank back the net panel at the window to get a better look. I zero in on a lone gray camper truck nosed into the chain-link fence. "Adele!" I rasp. "Come here! Hurry!"

She yawns before padding over to join me. "What is it? Please tell me the car's still intact."

I jab a finger at the windowpane. "Look! Over there by the chain-link fence. Do you see it? Is that the same camper truck we saw on the highway yesterday?" I scratch the back of my hand nervously, a cold sweat forming like a film over the nape of my neck.

Adele frowns as she peers through the window. "I'm ... not sure. I don't remember seeing that large blue cooler bungee-corded to the back."

"We wouldn't have been able to see that. The camper truck was behind us the whole way."

"Except at the Chevron station in Barstow," Adele says. "Do you remember if it had a cooler attached?"

I rack my brain, but I can't be sure. The truth is, I wasn't paying that much attention to the other vehicles. My attention was focused on the elderly man who'd collapsed. "Forget the cooler," I say. "CJ could have picked that up along the way. Now's our chance to find out if that's his truck. Let's run down there and take a closer look before too many people are out and about. We can take some pictures—that way we'll have a license plate. If it shows up again, then we'll know for sure someone's following us."

Adele throws me a dubious look. "I don't think that's such a good idea. What if Gianna and CJ are waiting for us? They might be hiding in the back of the camper."

"What if they are?" I throw my hands up in exasperation. " It's not as if they can abduct us from a hotel parking lot. And what if you've got it all wrong, and Gianna's tied up inside?"

Adele presses her lips into a thin line of disapproval. "I don't like it. We should forget about Gianna and get out of here."

"Fine. Don't come down with me if you don't want to," I say testily, as I turn on my heel.

I make a mad dash to the bathroom, before pulling some wrinkled clothes out of my case and getting dressed. Ordinarily, I like to take my time putting together my outfits so they photograph well, but I'm desperate to get down to the parking lot before the camper takes off. Despite my ambivalence about Gianna, I won't be able to live with myself if I hear on the news later that her body was found dumped along the I-40.

"Wait for me!" Adele says, hurriedly stuffing her belongings into her suitcase. "If you're determined to check it out, I'll go with you. Let's take our stuff and get back on the road afterward."

We ride the elevator down with several other guests departing early. My heart is thudding so loudly in my chest, I'm half afraid they'll be able to hear it reverberating off the elevator walls. I don't know if I'm doing the right thing. The worst part is that I don't know for sure if Gianna needs our help, or if she's a threat—or neither. I keep oscillating between wanting to believe her story of abuse at CJ's hands and suspecting her of participating in a scheme to defraud us. Clay's right about my naïveté. I'm not good at reading people's true intentions. I'm far too trusting for my own good.

Adele and I load our bags into the Tahoe and then gingerly make our way across the parking lot to the chain-link fence at the back of the hotel where the camper truck is parked. The truck body is a silver gray, just like the one we saw on the highway, and Adele's convinced that was the color of the camper truck in Barstow. I steal an uneasy glance around the deserted space. Only a handful of vehicles are parked in this area at the back of the hotel—trucks and vans, for the most part. We walk up to the grimy camper truck and peer cautiously through the driver's side window.

It's filthy and cluttered inside. It almost looks as though someone's been living in it. I try the driver's door but, unsurprisingly, it's locked.

Adele peers apprehensively over her shoulder. "Heads up," she hisses. "There are some people walking out to their RV. Pretend you're looking at your phone or something."

After the RV has driven off, I resume my inspection of the camper truck. I'm not tall enough to see in through the small side windows of the camper shell, which is frustrating because that's likely where Gianna would be if CJ's holding her hostage. I stare at the dust-covered cooler attached to the back of the camper with a pair of crisscrossed bungee cords. "Do you see that?" I say to Adele, swallowing hard as I gesture to a dark rust-colored stain on one side of the cooler.

"Is it blood?" she asks in a hushed tone.

"I don't know, but I think we should take a look inside." Tentatively, I raise my hand to unhook one of the bungee cords. A shuffling sound behind me stops me in my tracks.

"Looking for me?" a rough voice booms in my ear.

13

I spin around and stare at the disheveled figure limping up to the camper truck. His clothes are dirt-encrusted, and his right foot is encased in an orthopedic boot that looks like it's been marched through a battlefield or two. A matted beard hangs over his chest like a frayed bib that's gone gray with too many washes.

"I'm ... sorry," I say, raising my hands in a contrite gesture. "My friend and I mistook your camper for someone else's."

Adele nods, twisting her hands sheepishly in front of her.

"Sure you did," the man scoffs angrily as he shuffles up to the driver's door. His beady eyes dart up and down the length of me. "Caught you in the act, more like it."

He dismisses us with a disgusted shake of his head before unlocking the camper and clambering in. Without another word, he slams the door shut and gives an obnoxious rev of the engine, sending a plume of black smoke out the exhaust.

Adele and I waste no time retreating to the Tahoe, chastened and shaken by the encounter.

A shiver of revulsion ripples through me as I fasten my seatbelt. "He spooked me half to death, but at least that derelict wasn't CJ."

Adele grimaces. "He looked like he'd crawled out of a cave somewhere."

I start up the engine and grip the steering wheel. "Do you think we should follow him for a few miles, just in case?"

Adele throws me an irritated look. "In case *what*? He's got to be at least sixty years old, and he's hobbling along in a foot cast. He's obviously not Gianna's jerk boyfriend. It wasn't the same camper that was behind us on the highway. This whole situation has made us paranoid."

"Maybe I am being paranoid," I say, backing out of the parking spot. "But that guy sure looked like the serial killer type. What if he knocked CJ and Gianna off and stole their truck? I'd feel better if we'd gotten a look inside that cooler."

"I'm glad we didn't!" Adele retorts. "Didn't you notice his camo seat covers? I bet he's got meat in that cooler from a hunting trip."

"Let's hope that's all that's in there," I respond glumly.

"I'd put money on it. Let's just forget all about cranky camo guy and seize the day," Adele says, one corner of her lips quirking into a shaky grin. "I don't want to talk about camper trucks anymore, or waste one more minute thinking about Gianna. We tried to help her, and she left us high and dry. She walked out of the hotel of her own accord—it's time we put the whole encounter behind us."

"You're right," I agree, resigning myself to closing the topic for now. It's not fair to Adele to allow the rest of our trip to be consumed by Gianna's drama. Yet, as I settle in for the drive to Oklahoma City, my mind is still sifting through the past couple of days, trying to make sense of her disappearance. I have a nagging feeling that someone's in danger, but I can't decide if it's her or me.

After purchasing our tickets for the Oklahoma City National Memorial and Museum, Adele and I, along with a group of other visitors, are ushered into a darkened room. We take our seats on wooden benches stationed around the perimeter, a forbidding silence falling over us. All eyes are on the empty chairs surrounding the dimly lit conference table in the center of the room. After a moment or two, a recording of a Water Board meeting commences from the conference speaker in the middle of the table. As the monotonous meeting gets underway, my heart begins to thud in anticipation. April 19, 1995 was just another day on the job. No one in the building could have anticipated that their lives would end at 9:02 a.m., or, at the very least, be forever altered physically, mentally, and emotionally.

I squirm in my seat, bracing myself as the minutes on the clock tick by in ominous expectation. Even though I know what's about to happen, the thunderous boom of the explosion, when it comes, makes me flinch so hard my heart almost bursts through my chest. Gasps discharge all around the room like bullets. A low murmuring breaks out as people whisper to one another in reverential tones. Shaking like a leaf, I get to my feet, along with everyone else, and exit the room into the next part of the museum. "That was terrifyingly lifelike!" I say to Adele, resting one hand on my chest as my breathing slowly ratchets down a notch.

She gives a somber nod. "I can't imagine living through something like that. One minute you're going about your job, and the next thing you know, you're fleeing for your life —dripping blood and digging your way out through bodies and rubble."

"It's horrific," I say, shaking my head as I walk over to read a placard in front of an exhibit enclosed in glass. It turns out to be an actual room in the Federal building that was partially demolished in the bombing. "Look at this, Adele. It says here the blast was so big that three-hundred-and-forty-seven buildings across the city were damaged. That's worse than war."

We make our way along a glass corridor to the next room, stopping to stare through the window at an outdoor memorial comprising a field of empty chairs on the other side of a rectangular reflecting pool. "There's exactly one-hundred-and-sixty-eight of them—nineteen kid-sized," I say. "My neighbor told me they light them up at night." I press my lips tightly together, tears unexpectedly stinging my eyes.

"This place reminds me of the holocaust museum," Adele comments, as we pass between glass cases full of abandoned shoes, reading glasses, wallets, and keys retrieved from the rubble.

I frown at a tiny boot atop a pile of battered shoes. "How can anyone justify blowing up innocent children—for any cause?"

"It's a whole other level of evil," Adele agrees, with a shudder.

"Check this out. It's Timothy McVeigh's actual getaway car," I say, walking over to the acrylic railing cordoning off the infamous Easter-yellow 1977 Mercury Grand Marquis.

"He didn't get very far," Adele observes, studying the

placard next to the car. "It says he was pulled over by a state trooper an hour-and-a-half after the bombing for driving without a license plate. The trooper spotted a Glock handgun under his jacket and ended up arresting him for carrying an illegal concealed weapon. Lucky break for the authorities."

I nod, but I'm only half listening. My attention has been diverted by a tall, unshaven figure wearing a baseball cap and a black leather jacket. I noticed him earlier in the reenactment room, and now that I think about it, I've spotted him in almost every exhibit hall we've been in. He always seems to be standing off to one side with his face tilted away from us, but he's taking our exact route through the museum. A chill snakes its way up my spine. I nudge Adele discreetly and motion with my chin in his direction.

She frowns and turns to whisper to me, "What about him?"

"I think he might be tailing us. He keeps showing up at every exhibit we're at."

"You're being paranoid again," Adele replies. "Look around you. This is the same group of people we started the tour with."

"I've got a bad feeling about him. Let's find a restroom and disappear for a few minutes," I insist.

Adele shrugs indifferently. "If it makes you feel better."

I waste no time making a bee line for the nearest restroom. Safely inside, I lean back against the sink and take a quick calming breath.

"I don't know why you're so worried about him," Adele says, turning to look at herself in the mirror. "He was in our group from the beginning. Are you thinking it could be CJ?"

I shrug. "I don't know. I didn't get a good look at him at

the gas station with the sunglasses and baseball cap he had on."

"Me neither," she says, pulling out a coral lip gloss. "We'll hang out here for a few minutes and let that guy go ahead of us, just to ease your mind."

I check my phone for messages but there's nothing from Clay. He's probably still mad at me for being *evasive* as he called it. I don't feel like dealing with him right now. I'll try and smooth things over later when I'm not so agitated. I check my Instagram feed, and respond to several comments, before Adele finally says, "Let's get going. That should be long enough for him to move on."

To my relief, the man is nowhere in sight when we return to the exhibit hall. We resume our tour through the remainder of the museum, and then approach the exit where we get in line behind an elderly couple to sign the guest book on our way out. After adding our names to the thousands of others who've paid their respects, we file silently through the exit door leading to the museum store. I freeze when I spot the man again, looking through a display of books. I nudge Adele in the ribs. "It's him! He might be waiting for us."

Adele lets out an exasperated sigh. "Trust me, it's not CJ. The way Gianna described him, he'd sooner bury bodies in the desert than visit a museum." Before I can protest, she grabs me by the elbow and steers me straight over to a rack of postcards next to the book display the man is perusing.

He looks through a couple of books, and then turns to a blonde woman standing a short distance away and exchanges a few words with her. The pent-up tension inside me instantly deflates—they're talking in Italian, tourists, no doubt. "Sorry!" I mouth to Adele who's eying me with a petulant expression.

"You can't keep doing this for the rest of the trip, you know," she says, moving briskly in the direction of the main exit.

"Doing what?" I ask, although I know perfectly well what she's getting at.

She flicks her curls over her shoulder in an irritated manner. "Suspecting everyone of stalking us."

"So I'm just supposed to ignore it when I have a gut feeling that something's not right?" I ask, in an overly sharp tone.

"Maybe you should give it a try now and again." Adele arches a brow at me. "You thought that hunter's camper was CJ's, and you just suspected an Italian tourist of being him."

"So you don't like me being cautious, all of a sudden?" I retort. "You've changed your tune. You were the one who was afraid CJ was coming after us this whole time."

"Yes, but Gianna's not with us anymore. Why would CJ want to follow us now?" She hesitates and softens her tone. "Look, I'm just suggesting that you take it down a notch."

"That's not what I told you when you were afraid. I tried to be patient even when you weren't being rational," I snap back, before turning and stomping down the museum steps. My stomach churns as I walk across the parking lot to the car. I've already fallen out with my husband, and now I'm arguing with my best friend on what was supposed to be the trip of a lifetime. I have Gianna to thank for this mess. It's the last time I help out a stranger.

The atmosphere in the car is unbearably frosty when we get back on the road. Adele turns on the audiobook and we let *Big Little Lies* play uninterrupted for close to an hour without either of us venturing to say a word. I'm not really paying attention to the plot. I'm busy trying to decide what counts as a big little lie—or, if there is even such a thing.

Shading the truth, perhaps? My mind flits to the unsettling sketch in Gianna's notebook. *One of us won't survive this road trip. Kill or be killed.* Was that a lie, or did she know something we don't? If she was right about CJ killing his previous girlfriend, what's to stop him from striking again?

By the time we arrive at the Fairfield Inn in Little Rock, Arkansas, later that afternoon, Adele and I have managed to put our spat behind us. We get out of the car laughing hysterically while reminiscing about the first trip we took together to Mexico where everything that could go wrong, did go wrong. "We were halfway to the airport when you realized you'd forgotten your passport," I choke out, weeping tears of laughter. "We had to rebook our flight for the next day, and you got to sit beside that hot male Brazilian model."

Adele holds her stomach, laughing uproariously. "Except the flight was so turbulent I threw up on his Nike sneakers! I didn't make a great impression."

"Remember our first morning there? We were woken up by the radio alarm in our room blasting heavy metal music," I say, honking with laughter as I drag our luggage out of the car. "You twisted your ankle jumping out of bed trying to yank the cord from the wall." I lean back against the Tahoe and hold my stomach, laughing so hard that every muscle hurts. "The best part was when you slipped and fell in the pool in front of that bachelor party."

Adele lets out a snort. "How about when you got locked in the bathroom stall at the Cactus Amigos restaurant and the toothless maintenance guy had to climb in and rescue you?"

Still giggling under the curious glances of the other guests, we wheel our cases inside the hotel foyer. I hand Adele my credit card. "You check us in. I don't think I can keep a straight face," I say.

"What's your license plate?" she calls to me from the reception desk.

I rattle it off, almost choking in the process as I try not to succumb to another fit of giggles.

The concierge arches a discreet brow in my direction as she punches in the information and codes our keys.

Inside our room on the second floor, we collapse on the beds and laugh some more. It's such a relief to release the tension that has built up over the past few days. I'm only realizing now how much of a cloud Gianna cast over us when she was with us.

"I needed that," I say, sitting up and drying my eyes.

"We both did," Adele agrees. "And now I need food. I'm starving. I can only eat so much trail mix before I turn into a chipmunk."

AFTER DINNER and a good night's sleep, I'm ready to hit the road again, determined to put all thoughts of CJ and the camper truck out of my mind.

We shower up and are just about to head out the door when the phone in our room rings.

I hesitate and exchange a bemused look with Adele.

"Leave it," she says impatiently. "It can't be for us."

I shrug and exit the room after her, but a flicker of unease goes through me, nonetheless.

There's a crowd of people waiting on the elevator, so we take the stairs down instead and make our way to the foyer. Two police officers are standing at the concierge desk talking to the woman who checked us in. When she spots us, she gestures toward us with a subtle tilt of her head. The officers glance over at us and immediately stride across the foyer in our direction.

The tall, clean-shaven cop looks directly at me. "Cora Lewis?"

My skin prickles as I try to read the expression on his face. I part my lips to answer but my tongue is stuck to the roof of my mouth. In the pit of my stomach, I fear the worst.

14

———

"Yes, I'm Cora Lewis," I stammer, my eyes darting between the two officers.

Adele shoots me a terrified look. She's got to be thinking the same thing I am—that Gianna has turned up dead and we're the prime suspects in her murder. Two officers wearing grim expressions can only mean bad news. I squeeze the strap of my purse tightly as I sift through my panicked thoughts. How did the police know Gianna was traveling with us? Surely her father wouldn't have reported her missing already—we're not due in Nashville until tomorrow. Maybe I'm jumping the gun, and this has nothing to do with Gianna at all. My pulse quickens as a worse possibility hits me like a thunderbolt. I take a quick breath, stumbling over my words, "Is ... is my husband okay?"

The officer clears his throat. "We're not here about your husband, ma'am. Perhaps we can talk in private for a few minutes." He gestures to a door behind the reception desk. "The manager has allowed us the use of her office."

I try to ignore the curious glances of the other hotel guests as Adele and I follow the police into a stuffy, windowless room. My legs feel like elastic as I walk past a desk over-flowing with stacks of files and paperwork. I sink down on a sagging couch at the back of the cramped room, my thoughts hurtling several steps ahead of me. If this has nothing to do with Clay, then it must be about Gianna. I should have trusted Adele's judgement—she's my best friend for a reason. It was a mistake to get mixed up with a stranger, especially one who admitted from the outset to having a dangerous boyfriend. I could kick myself for being so naive and stubborn, it's a dangerous combination. Who knows what all CJ and Gianna were involved in. Adele and I might be implicated in a crime spree we know nothing about. Whatever they've done, we're an inadvertent link in the chain at this point.

I hunch over in my seat, my stomach cramping as the officers fetch a couple of folding chairs and set them up opposite us.

"Do you think this is about Gianna?" Adele whispers in my ear.

I shrug. There's no time to answer her question before the officers take their seats and turn their attention to us. The taller one pulls out a small black notebook and flicks it open in one deft movement, eying us all the while with an expression that gives nothing away. "I'm Officer Myers and this is my partner, Officer Wade."

"What's this about?" Adele asks, a hint of defiance in her tone. I can't blame her for copping an attitude. So far, the coast-to-coast trip of a lifetime I promised her isn't panning out how I envisioned it. It's edging closer to a full-blown Thelma-and-Louise catastrophe. It was humiliating being escorted into the manager's office like a pair of criminals, under the gob-smacked stares of the other hotel guests. They probably thought we'd been caught with a stash of

Comfort Inn towels in our suitcases or something along those lines. If only that were the case.

"We appreciate your cooperation," Officer Myers begins. "We have a few questions for you about Gianna Halstead."

I wet my lips nervously as I wait for him to elaborate. He didn't lead by telling us she's dead, which leaves me cautiously optimistic. It's the first time I've heard her last name, but she's the only Gianna I know.

"Is she in some kind of trouble?" Adele asks, trying, and failing, to sound unconcerned. She might as well have asked outright if we were in some kind of trouble—which I'm certain we are. A wave of shame prickles my face. Clay is going to be furious when he finds out the mess I've got us into.

"She's been reported as missing," Officer Myers explains.

My pulse thuds in my dry throat. I could have told him that. As far as I know, Adele and I were the last two people to see Gianna before she disappeared. I wonder who reported her missing. I doubt it was CJ. If he was as abusive as she claimed, he wouldn't want to draw attention to himself.

"Her father gave us your phone number," Officer Wade chimes in, as if reading the question in my mind. "We pinged your phone to locate you."

"I understand you're on your way to New York. What's the purpose of your trip?" Officer Myers asks.

"My grandmother passed away and I inherited her house in Katonah," I reply. "I have to sign the paperwork and clean the place out so I can list it."

"Gianna's father tells us you agreed to give her a ride as far as Nashville," Officer Myers says. "Is she a friend of yours?" He looks artlessly from me to Adele, but the question is anything but innocent. I'm well aware that all options are on the table at this point, as far as he's concerned. For all he knows, we could have robbed Gianna, killed her, and dumped her body somewhere along the way.

I straighten up in my seat. "We didn't know her. She ... hitched a ride with us but she left us in Albuquerque—took off early from the hotel we were staying at."

Officer Myers cocks his head to one side, his bristly eyebrows shooting up in surprise. "Are you in the habit of picking up hitchhikers?"

I open my mouth to respond, but before I can think of a delicate way to explain the situation, Adele blurts out, "We didn't pick her up. She stowed away in our car at a gas station in Barstow. She hid under our luggage. We had no clue she was back there until we reached Kingman, several hours later. She fed us a sob story about running away from her abusive boyfriend." Adele hesitates and throws me an apologetic look. "I ... didn't want to take her with us—she gave me the creeps. I wasn't even sure her story was true, but Cora guilted me into agreeing to it."

Officer Myers consults his notebook. "We have an address for her parents in Nashville, so that part of her story checks out. Apparently, her father was expecting her to arrive there yesterday."

"We didn't guarantee any particular date," I interrupt. "We won't be there until tomorrow."

Officer Myers scribbles something down. "He was concerned because she was traveling with a friend he'd never heard her talk about before. He's been trying to call her, but he can't get a response."

"She didn't have her phone with her," I explain. "She told us her boyfriend took it."

Officer Myers scratches his chin. "Do you have any idea where she went?"

"No," I reply. "She walked out of the hotel about four in the morning and never came back—the manager showed us the security footage. We waited around for a few hours to make sure she didn't show back up."

"She stole my iPad," Adele adds, jutting out her chin. "Probably took it straight to a pawn shop."

Officer Myers frowns and makes a note of it. "Was anyone with her, or did she seem distressed in any way?"

I shake my head. "She was alone. She had her backpack with her, so we figured she'd decided to go back to her ex and was too embarrassed to tell us."

A furrow forms on Officer Myers' brow. "Why would she be embarrassed about that?"

"He was a loser, and she knew it," Adele cuts in. "He wouldn't let her have her phone, or her wallet. He talked her into taking a camping trip into the desert—supposedly, to hunt for treasure. His previous girlfriend went missing a year or so ago, and Gianna was scared he was planning to knock her off too."

Officer Myers exchanges a meaningful look with his partner, before jotting down some more notes. "Do you know her boyfriend's name?"

"CJ," I reply. "I don't know his last name. He drives a beat-up camper truck. We saw him once at the Chevron station in Barstow."

"I don't suppose you know the license plate—or what state it was issued in?"

I shrug. "No clue. I was helping an elderly man who'd collapsed in the heat. We had to wait for an ambulance. I wasn't paying much attention to the other vehicles at the station. That's how Gianna was able to slip into our car unnoticed."

"How about the camper make or color?" Officer Myers prods.

I scratch my forehead. "I thought the truck was white, but Adele remembers it as being gray. It was so dirty it's hard to say for sure."

"I think CJ was following us on the I-40 at one point," Adele adds. "We exited and thought we'd managed to lose him, but he might have tracked us down to the hotel in Albuquerque. If you're looking for Gianna, you might want to start by finding him."

Officer Myers gives a grim nod. "We'll pursue that line of inquiry. I'll also need to take a look at that footage you mentioned. Do you have the name and address of the hotel you stayed at in Albuquerque?"

I dig around in my purse for the hotel manager's business card and pass it to him.

In return, he hands me his card. "Please call me right away if Gianna gets in contact with you, or if you think of anything else that might be useful. We may be in touch again if we have any follow-up questions. Enjoy the rest of your trip, ladies."

I get to my feet and hesitate. "You ... will let us know when you find her, won't you?"

The expression on Officer Myers' face softens momentarily. He gives a curt nod. "You can count on it."

Adele and I make our way out to the Tahoe in subdued silence. I'm still reeling from the encounter with the officers. They didn't hint at any suspicions they might harbor about our involvement in Gianna's disappearance, but something tells me they'll be keeping tabs on us for the rest of the trip. If they suspect us of having a hand in something nefarious, the last thing they're going to do is alert us to the fact.

"That was a bit of a downer to start our day on," Adele

says, as she backs out of our parking spot, running over the curb in the process.

I flinch at the clumsy maneuver but bite my tongue. I don't want to tick her off and be forced to drive in stony silence for the next few hours again. "Do you think the police suspect us of doing something to Gianna?"

"Of course not!" Adele scoffs. "It's obvious she went skulking back to CJ. The cops are just going through the motions to satisfy her father. Forget about it. It's over and done with. Next stop, Graceland, Memphis."

I frown out my window at a middle-aged woman standing by the hotel entrance who's pointing us out to her companions. No doubt, they're speculating on the nature of our small-time criminal offenses. I turn away, not wanting to give them the satisfaction of seeing the turmoil on my face. Adele's right—we just need to make the best of the situation. There's nothing more we can do. At least the police are involved now. I have to believe that if something's happened to Gianna, they'll get to the bottom of it. I pull up the playlist we made of Elvis's greatest hits and click on *Heartbreak Hotel*. After the humiliating interview in the Comfort Inn, it seems like a fitting note to kick off our Memphis leg of the trip with.

Two-and-a-half hours later, Adele and I are standing outside Graceland Mansion, the King of Rock 'n' Roll's private retreat, taking another batch of selfies. I've been looking forward to this stop, and I'm determined not to waste a minute of it agonizing over Gianna's whereabouts.

"I think it's really sweet that Elvis moved his parents into Graceland with him," I say, as we wander along a hallway chockfull of black and white family photos documenting his humble beginnings. "Imagine going from being dirt poor to being the parents of one of the wealthiest people in the world."

"I didn't know Elvis had a twin!" Adele exclaims, as she stops to read a placard on the wall. "It's so sad that his brother was stillborn. Kind of funny their mother didn't know she was having twins until Elvis popped out thirty-five minutes later."

"Yay for ultrasounds!" I say, as we exit the exhibit hall.

Along with the rest of our group, we continue our tour through Elvis's automobile and career museum packed with cars, memorabilia, custom jumpsuits, and some of his most iconic stage costumes. I'm blown away by the hundreds of personal artifacts and photos depicting his incredible life and legacy—everything from his iconic pink Cadillac to his personal fleet of airplanes.

"Can you believe the gold-plated seatbelts?" Adele says, shaking her head in disbelief as we walk through the customized 1958 Convers 880 jet named Lisa Marie after Elvis's only child.

"I remember reading somewhere that he flew to Colorado one afternoon with Lisa Marie just to let her play in the snow for a couple of hours," I say. "Can you imagine that kind of lifestyle?"

"It's so sad how he ended up," Adele says. "Just goes to show that money can't buy happiness."

"Are you sure about that?" I ask, jabbing her playfully in the ribs. "My money's buying us this miserable trip."

Adele gives a tight grin but says nothing. I can't help thinking that she regrets agreeing to come on the trip with me. The whole incident with Gianna has left a sour taste in our mouths, but it's not too late to put it behind us and make the most of the rest of our time together. And that's exactly what I intend to do.

"Ready to find a hotel?" I ask when we exit the plane exhibit. "My feet are killing me. I need to rest up before we hit the Country Music Hall of Fame tomorrow."

Adele grins. "Now *that's* going to be the highlight of the trip for me."

"I don't know about all that country music," I respond with a chuckle. "Too much heartache and bellyaching for me."

My phone rings as I'm unlocking the car in the parking lot. I glance at it, relieved it's not Clay. The secrets I'm keeping from him are beginning to wear me down like a ball and chain. He'd blow a gasket if he knew I'd been interviewed by the police today.

I don't recognize the number on the screen, but it could be Officer Myers, so I take the call.

"Hello?" I say, as I slide into the passenger seat.

"Murderer!" a voice growls.

15

M y hand begins to shake so hard I almost drop the phone. I don't recognize the voice. Is it Gianna's father? Have they found her body? Surely he doesn't think I had anything to do with whatever happened to her after she left the hotel. "Who ... who is this?" I manage to squeak out.

Adele glances across at me, her eyes widening at the trepidation in my expression. "What's wrong?" she whispers.

I give a firm shake of my head and put the phone on speaker so she can hear everything. "Who is this?" I repeat more loudly.

"Where's Gianna?" the man on the other end of the line yells. "What did you do to my girlfriend?"

Adele and I exchange a loaded look. My heart convulses in my chest. *CJ!* How did he get my number?

"I could ask you the same question," I reply, trying desperately to stop my voice from quavering. "We know you've been following us. You met up with Gianna at the gas station in Gallup, didn't you?"

I wait for him to deny it, but dead silence fills the car.

"Why were you following us?" Adele asks.

"I'm only gonna ask you one more time. Where ... is ... she?" CJ repeats, his voice low and threatening.

"We don't know," I reply, tamping down my exasperation. "She left our hotel in Albuquerque without saying a word to anyone. We figured she'd decided to run back to you."

"If you've hurt her, I swear I'll—"

"We didn't do anything to her," I retort, cutting him off. "Look, I was just trying to do your girlfriend a favor by giving her a ride to Nashville. For some reason, she decided to bail on us. I don't want any part of your dysfunctional relationship. Obviously, she doesn't want to be with you anymore, so get over it. She's an adult, she has every right to go wherever she wants to without you trying to control her every move."

"You don't know what you're talking about," CJ growls. "She would never leave me. Something's happened to her, and I know you're involved, so you'd better start talking."

"Don't threaten me," I yell. "I'm hanging up now, and if you keep stalking us, I'm calling the police." I promptly end the call and hunch forward on my seat, scrunching my eyes shut. The situation is mushrooming out of control. What if CJ convinces the police we had something to do with Gianna's disappearance? I don't know how much she told him about us. He probably knows that Adele and Gianna didn't get along all that well—couldn't stand each other, if I'm being honest. He could use that against us.

"It's all right," Adele soothes, squeezing my shoulder. "He's just mad because Gianna didn't go running back to him. She likely realized he'd been following us and decided it would be better to disappear quietly. I bet CJ just wanted to make sure we weren't hiding her from him. I'm pretty sure he won't bother us anymore."

"I'm calling Officer Myers and letting him know CJ threatened us," I say, fumbling in my purse for the number.

Adele frowns. "What if CJ tells him we had something to do with Gianna's disappearance? It's his word against ours. It doesn't help that she was with us when she went missing."

I groan as I straighten up in my seat. "I'm sorry for not listening to you when you tried to talk sense into me. I know I'm pig-headed when I get a notion about something. Clay would have told me the same thing you did, but I honestly thought Gianna was being abused."

"You're just too nice a person, that's all," Adele says.

"Naive, you mean." I give her a rueful grin as I start up the engine. "Crazy morning, huh? Hopefully, that's the last we hear from CJ. If he threatens us again, I'm reporting him to the police—I don't care what he tells them."

"Let's put it behind us," Adele says. "What's next on the agenda?"

"I'd like to visit the Civil Rights Museum in the morning before we leave Memphis, and then blast off to Nashville tomorrow and hit the Country Music Hall of Fame—seems appropriate to wallow in some woe-is-me music now that we've run into all this trouble."

"No kidding," Adele agrees, pulling out her phone. "Speaking of country music, I reckon it's time for some Miranda Lambert." She selects a song from our playlist and connects it to the car stereo. She darts a grin my way. "Nashville tomorrow, girl! I can't wait to break in my new cowboy boots."

I force myself to smile back at her, quashing the feeling that the circumstances surrounding Gianna's disappearance are darker than either of us can imagine. "You might want to start looking for a hotel," I remind her.

"I'm on it. Do you want city center or closer to the highway?"

"Let's go city center so we can walk to Beale Street and check out the music scene later if we feel like it."

Adele scrolls for several minutes, frowning in concentration. "Oh wow, the Peabody Hotel looks gorgeous. It's on the National Register of Historic Places. It's world-famous for its five resident ducks who march through the lobby to the fountain every day at 11:00 a.m. and back out at 5:00 p.m."

"You're kidding me!" I say incredulously. "We have to see that."

Adele angles a brow at me. "At three-hundred dollars a night that place is most definitely not in our budget. But it's only a few miles from here. If we hurry, we can watch the duck march and then go find ourselves a fleabag motel to camp out in."

I chuckle. "At least we haven't had to spend a night in the car yet. Give me some directions to this famous duck lodge."

After parking in the overpriced self-parking lot at the Peabody Hotel, Adele and I make our way inside.

My jaw drops as I take in the cavernous foyer with its elaborate architecture and chandeliers. "Wow! This place is stunning!" I exclaim, my gaze traveling over the enormous fountain cut from travertine marble stationed in the center of the lobby. "Look at that gorgeous flower display!"

"Aw, check out the ducks, they're so cute," Adele says, as we make our way toward the fountain. We merge with the crowd that has gathered to watch the show. Minutes later, the elevator doors in the lobby slide open and a man steps out, dressed in an elegant red jacket and holding a cane. He rolls out a red carpet all the way up to the fountain before introducing himself as the Peabody Duckmaster.

"Tradition has it," he bellows out, looking around like a

circus master intent on engaging the crowd, "that back in the 1930s, the General Manager of The Peabody and his good friend returned from a hunting trip after having indulged in a little too much Tennessee whiskey. For a lark, they decided to put a few of their live duck decoys in the magnificent Peabody fountain that you see before you." The Duckmaster gestures at it with an elaborate flourish. "When the two men woke the following morning in a more sober state of mind, they hurried downstairs to remove the ducks before anyone raised a ruckus, only to discover that the hotel guests were enamored by them. And so, ladies and gentlemen, a world-renowned Peabody tradition began." He pauses and peers down at several wide-eyed children standing behind the velvet rope separating us from the red carpet. "Now, it's time for the Peabody duck march to commence."

He taps his cane on the edge of the fountain and immediately the strains of a lively waltz are piped throughout the foyer. The Duckmaster marches all the way around the fountain, holding his cane out to gather the ducks to the front. One by one, they jump up onto the ledge and waggle their way down the red carpet toward the open elevator.

"Can you believe it?" Adele whispers, her eyes glistening.

I glance around at the mesmerized crowd. Everyone, from elementary-aged kids to gray-haired men in business suits, is captivated by the endearing sight of a duck processional. It's a heartwarming reminder of how innocent the world can be despite the darkness lurking in every corner. A shiver darts across my shoulders. I really believed Gianna had snuck out of the hotel in Albuquerque to rejoin CJ. But, after his phone call, I'm more worried than ever that something's happened to her. My mind goes back to her ominous diary entry predicting someone's death.

"Ready to get out of here?" Adele asks, as the crowd begins to disperse.

I turn to look at her, face all aglow. She's made a lot of sacrifices to accompany me to New York, and I promised her the trip of a lifetime. It's time I did something to make up for all the unpleasantness I've subjected her to. "We're not going anywhere," I say impulsively. "We're spending the night here."

Adele's eyes crinkle in confusion. "What do you mean? It's far too expensive."

I shrug. "That's for me to decide. We can indulge for one night—courtesy of the grandmother I never met."

I leave Adele standing open-mouthed in the middle of the lobby and make my way up to the gleaming reception counter. I've never in my life paid three-hundred dollars for a hotel room, but I manage to hand over my credit card in a composed fashion, as though the exorbitant sum doesn't faze me.

"Will you be needing help with your luggage this evening, Ms. Lewis?" the concierge asks in a polished tone.

I bat my hand dismissively. "No, that's all right, thanks. It's still in the car. I'll get it later."

The concierge nods and hands me two key cards. She motions like a flight attendant over my shoulder. "The elevators are behind you and the stairs are to the left. Please let us know if there's anything else we can do to make your stay more enjoyable, Ms. Lewis."

"Thank you ... I will," I stammer, suddenly overcome by her silky tone and the opulent surroundings.

I scuttle back to Adele who's still standing transfixed by the fountain. "We're officially guests of The Peabody," I announce with a jubilant air. "Let's go get our bags. I think we can safely leave our pillows in the car for one night."

Ensconced in our luxurious room, we explore our surroundings like a couple of high schoolers, oohing and aahing over the sumptuous, pillowed seating, elegant light fixtures, and carved wooden headboards that resemble something out of a château. "Now we're talking!" I say, testing out the pillows. "I feel like my head's floating on a cloud."

"I could get used to this," Adele exclaims, falling backward on one of the beds, arms outstretched.

In the bathroom, I test some of the expensive-looking products and admire the Carrara marble tile. It's a far cry from the moldy bathroom in the hotel we stayed at in Albuquerque.

"What do you want to do for dinner?" Adele asks, when I walk back out to unpack my bag.

"We're in Memphis so we have to eat barbecue," I reply. "Isn't that what they're famous for?"

"Absolutely! Barbecue capital of the world," Adele confirms, getting to her feet. "I'm going to change first. I need a cute outfit to rock the vibe."

"Time to debut our cowboy boots," I say without hesitation.

An hour later, we take our seats at a red checkered table in The Bar-B-Q Cafe.

"Smells like heaven," I say, inhaling the rich aroma of smoky barbecue sauce. "My stomach's rumbling."

"Have you seen the portions they serve?" Adele mutters in an awed tone, as she cranes to see the platter of food the couple at the next table is tucking into. "There's no way I can finish a mountain of food that size."

"I'm going with an order of ribs with hickory smoke-infused sweet 'n tangy sauce," I say, studying the menu. "How about you?"

"Same," Adele replies. "With cornbread and sides of beans and slaw."

My jaw drops when our orders arrive on plates the size of trays. The portions look even more enormous now that they're sitting on the table in front of us. The aroma of tantalizing spices kicks my taste buds into overdrive. I close my eyes and groan as I take the first mouthful—*sheer sticky deliciousness*. Several wads of napkins later, I push my plate to one side. "I'm done. I can't eat another mouthful."

"I'm never going to eat again," Adele declares, rubbing her belly.

"Great! You'll be a cheap date for the rest of the trip," I quip, as I sign the check. "Let's head back to our luxury accommodations so we can get the most out of my grandmother's money."

"My day to drive," Adele says, holding out her hand for the key.

As I follow her out to the parking lot at the back of the restaurant, my phone rings. I grimace, stopping in my tracks when I see that it's Clay. I could let it go to voicemail, but I'd only be delaying the inevitable. Maybe he's calling to apologize. I'm about to slide my finger across the screen to accept the call when I hear a muffled yelp.

I glance up in time to see a scruffy-looking man shoving Adele into the Tahoe.

16

"Adele!" I scream, breaking into a mad dash toward the Tahoe. The scruffy-looking man steals a glance in my direction before jumping into the passenger seat and slamming the door shut. When I reach the car, I wrench the handle on the driver's side and jiggle it feverishly, but it's locked. Adele turns her head slowly to look at me, her bulging eyes communicating what I fear most—*CJ has found us.*

I run around to the other side of the car and hammer on the window, yelling at him to open the door. He ignores me, his head close to Adele's as he whispers something in her ear. In desperation, I glance around the parking lot searching for someone to help me. A young couple, arms intertwined, are coming around the side of the restaurant and making their way to a car at the far end of the parking lot.

"Help me! Please!" I rasp, tugging desperately on the door handle. "He's locked the car!"

They throw a dubious look my way without breaking

their stride, no doubt dismissing my predicament as a lover's spat. Trembling, I scrabble around in my pocket for my phone, all the while keeping an eye out for anyone else who might be able to help me. The police will never get here in time. In all the movies I've watched, it only takes minutes to strangle someone to death. I've no idea what CJ's intentions are, but if he's killed before, he won't hesitate to do it again.

I'm about to dial 911 when a short, stocky man comes charging out of the restaurant. I wave frantically at him to get his attention. To my immense relief, he immediately changes course and starts striding toward me.

"Everything all right, sweetheart?" he asks, as he swaggers up to me. Up close, I can tell from the glassy look in his eyes and his ruddy complexion that he's had a fair amount to drink. But he looks like the type who's not afraid to inject himself into a situation, which is exactly what I need right now.

I jab at the Tahoe with my finger and stammer, "He's locked my friend inside my car."

The man puffs out his chest as he walks around to the passenger side and raps his knuckles on the window. To my surprise, CJ calmly rolls down the window and rests his elbow on it. "What's up?"

"This woman says you locked her friend in her car. What's going on, man?"

CJ gives an exaggerated shake of his head before motioning with his thumb in my direction. "That's my ex— she won't leave us alone." He turns to Adele. "Isn't that right, babe?"

Adele blinks and gives a tight-lipped smile. "Yes."

The stocky man slaps his palm on the roof of the car and straightens up. "Gotcha. You folks have a good night." He throws me a withering look and stomps off without another word.

"No! Wait! Please!" I call after him.

Ignoring my pleas, he jumps into his truck and peels out of the parking lot. With a mounting sense of panic, I turn my attention back to what's unfolding inside the Tahoe. The passenger door suddenly swings open and CJ climbs out. "You haven't heard the last from me," he snarls in my face, before stuffing his hands in his pockets and shoving past me. I watch him disappear around the street corner and then clamber into the car to check on Adele. "Are you okay? Did he hurt you?" I ask, reaching over to embrace her.

She rocks back-and-forth in her seat, her shoulders vibrating with fear. "I'm okay. I'm okay. I'm okay," she repeats, as though trying to reassure herself of the fact.

"Why did you lie to that man? He was trying to help us." I say.

Adele turns to me, her face drained of color. "CJ had a gun inside his jacket. He had it pointed at my stomach the whole time."

"What?" I yank my phone back out of my pocket. "I'm calling the police."

"No!" Adele grabs me by the wrist. "We can't. CJ warned me not to. He's concocted this whole story about how we threatened to kill Gianna. He's going to tell the cops he arranged to pick her up in Albuquerque, but she never showed. The police will think we had something to do with her disappearance."

I grimace. "What did CJ want?"

"He wanted to know where Gianna was. I told him we're as clueless as he is."

I rub a hand over my aching brow. "It doesn't make sense. If he did something to her, he wouldn't be pressing us for information. Maybe he really doesn't know where she is."

"He's unstable," Adele sobs. "Unstable people don't always make sense. Maybe he killed her and he's trying to cover his tracks by pinning it on us."

I slide my arm around her shoulder and pull her close. "It's all right. Don't cry. We'll figure this out. I'll drive us back to the hotel. You're in no state to be behind the wheel."

Safely back in the comfort of our room, I tuck Adele between the sheets and head into the bathroom to take a hot shower. Maybe in some subconscious way I'm trying to wash away the memory of CJ's snarling face, or maybe it's because I always think best standing under a pulsing stream of hot water. I need to sort out my swirling thoughts and figure out what's really going on. I was convinced CJ had done something to Gianna, but his actions aren't those of a man who killed his girlfriend. Which either means Gianna is hiding from him, or she's run into trouble at someone else's hand.

Frustrated, I step out of the shower and dry off with a luxurious bath towel. With an air of resignation, I sit down on the toilet lid to call Clay. It's time I fessed up to everything that's happened. It's bound to come out now, sooner or later. He'll be mad at me for being so reckless, but I need his perspective to help me figure out what to do.

My heart flutters in my chest as I wait for Clay to pick up. I'm feeling emotional after the attack on Adele—I only hope I don't burst into tears the minute I hear his voice. What happened in the parking lot was truly traumatic. I could have lost my best friend. Even if CJ didn't plan on harming Adele, the gun could have gone off accidentally. Or that stocky guy could have reached his fist inside the car and triggered a fight that might very well have ended in bloodshed. My insistence on playing the Good Samaritan with Gianna has put our lives at risk.

"Hey!" Clay says, sounding tentative but not angry anymore.

I take a quick breath before responding. "Hi, babe! Are we good? You're not still mad at me, are you?"

"No, of course not. I'm sorry for acting like a jerk. I was stressed out, that's all. I've been overloaded with work and studying till two or three in the morning most nights, so when you told me to go around and check on Jackson, it was the last straw."

"I'm sorry too," I say. "I didn't mean for you to get involved, it's not your problem."

"Okay, enough about that. It's forgotten. Where are you right now?"

"We're spending the night in Memphis. We're going to visit the Civil Rights Museum first thing in the morning and then drive to Nashville and hit the Country Music Hall of Fame."

"That's what Adele's most looking forward to, isn't it?" Clay says.

"So you *do* listen to what I have to say—some of the time, at least," I respond teasingly. "She's on cloud nine now that we're in cowboy country. We broke in our new boots tonight and went to dinner at this awesome barbecue joint—they had the best smoked ribs I've ever eaten."

"Sounds like the trip's going great," Clay says.

I tug my towel around myself a little tighter, summoning my courage. It's now or never. Time to come clean. "It's been amazing, for the most part."

"For the *most* part, what's that supposed to mean?" Clay asks, his tone switching to one of concern.

"Well, we had a bit of a situation."

"Is it the car? Let me guess, Adele was driving? We can get it fixed before my parents find out if that's what you're worried—"

"It's not the car," I interrupt.

"Then, what?"

"I'm trying to tell you, if you'd let me speak." I exhale a frustrated breath. "I know you said not to pick up anyone, but we offered to give this woman a ride—"

"What?" Clay explodes. "Absolutely not! You're not letting a stranger ride in the car with you."

"Too late. We already did."

Clay falls silent for a moment. I listen to his measured breathing, as he digests the news.

I wet my lips before continuing. "We picked her up in … Kingman, Arizona." I almost said Barstow but caught myself in time. Better not to mention that Gianna was hiding in our car for several hours, undetected. "She was supposed to go all the way to Nashville with us," I go on, "but she left the hotel we were staying at in Albuquerque in the early hours of the morning and we haven't seen her since. She's … missing."

"Missing? How do you know she's missing?" Clay asks, the undercurrent of disquiet in his tone rising rapidly. "Maybe she got a ride with someone else."

"No. She never showed up in Nashville. Her father reported her missing."

"She could have simply changed her mind," Clay says. "It's not a crime. Why's any of this your problem anyway?"

"Because the police tracked us down at our hotel and interviewed us."

"What?" Clay cries. "How did they know she was with you?"

"Gianna used my phone to call her father. He knew she was traveling with us."

"That's her name—Gianna? What's her last name?" Clay asks.

I huff out a breath. "What does it matter? You don't know her."

"How old is this woman?"

"She said she was nineteen, but I don't know if that's true —she looked young. I don't know how much of anything she told us was true, to be honest."

"So, she could have been a minor. What else did she tell you?" Clay demands.

"She said she was running away from her controlling boyfriend. He used to take her wallet and her phone—weird stuff like that. The really scary part is that his previous girl- friend went missing too, and Gianna was starting to suspect that he'd killed her."

I flinch at a loud clattering on the other end of the line. It sounds as if Clay's dropped something.

"Are you still there?" I venture.

"I just don't understand you, Cora!" he yells. "I don't know how many conversations we had about this trip, and what you should and shouldn't do, and how to avoid every danger out there. And then you turn around and do the stupidest thing you can possibly do when you're out on the road and pick up a hitchhiker."

I'm not about to correct him on the finer details of how exactly Gianna ended up in my car. It will only add fuel to the fire. "I was just trying to help the woman out, Clay. You know what a softie I am. I'm sorry—you were right. I should have listened to you."

"It isn't your problem anymore," Clay says, sounding

halfway mollified. "The police will deal with it now. She's probably just some runaway."

I chew on my lip for a moment. "Except it is still my problem because her boyfriend is harassing us."

"What do you mean by harassing?" Clay asks. "Is he calling your phone or something?"

I swallow the lump in my throat before answering. "It's worse than that. He's been following us in his camper truck. He was waiting for us when we came out of the restaurant this evening, and ... he confronted us." I pause for a breath, skipping over the fact that the confrontation involved taking Adele hostage at gunpoint. I'm feeling guiltier by the minute that I exposed my best friend to such a terrifying ordeal. "He thinks we had something to do with Gianna's disappearance."

"I can't believe this!" Clay growls. "Did you call the police?"

I hesitate for a nanosecond too long.

"Cora!" Clay yells into the phone. "I need to know if you called the police!"

"No. I'm pretty sure he won't bother us anymore. He just wanted to make sure Gianna wasn't with us." I close my eyes and picture CJ pressing the gun into Adele's side. I can't tell Clay the chilling truth—he might insist on flying out to Nashville and driving the rest of the way with us.

"I told you this trip was a bad idea," Clay says. "You should pack it in and come home."

"I'm not coming home. We're almost to Katonah now. I've made arrangements to meet the lawyer on Tuesday."

Clay sighs. "I don't want you driving back. Catch a return flight and ship the Tahoe. It's not like you won't be able to afford it once the house is yours."

I rub my eyes, overcome by tiredness. "We'll talk about it when I get there. It's late and I'm exhausted."

I hang up and crawl into bed, pulling the luxurious covers up to my neck. Everything is unbelievably soft and comfortable, and I feel like I'm sleeping on a cloud, but not even the opulent bedding is enough to let me sleep in peace. All I can see when I close my eyes is the gruesome profile of Adele's carved out face in Gianna's sketch.

One of us won't survive the road trip. Kill or be killed.

17

I wake with a start the following morning, shattered and wrung out from a night of troubled dreams: CJ breaking into our hotel room and holding us hostage with a machete, Gianna jumping out from behind him, laughing maniacally, Adele's face slowly melting into a puddle. Everything in me wants to pick up the phone and call the police to report CJ for assault. His words play on a continual loop in my brain: *You haven't heard the last from me.* Why would he say that? We already told him we don't know where Gianna is. The only thing I can think of is that he suspects we're helping her hide from him. If her stories of abuse are true, he knows we wouldn't willingly give away her location. If my hunch is right, there's a good chance CJ will continue to follow us—a thought that fills me with dread.

The issue nagging at me is where Gianna disappeared to. I was hoping, by now, she would have contacted me about getting her journal back, but maybe I was wrong about how attached she is to it. If CJ doesn't know her whereabouts, and her parents haven't heard from her either, it leaves the possibility that something too awful to contemplate has happened to her—something I might have unwittingly participated in. After all, I'm the one who brought her to a strange city, and we didn't end up staying in the safest part of town. Gianna might have gone out early to get some fresh air and stretch her legs before another long day in the car, and fallen victim to a mugging, or been attacked by some drunk—abducted even.

Adele stirs in her bed next to mine. "What time is it?" she mumbles.

"Almost seven," I say. "Time to rise and shine. We have a big day ahead of us. The Civil Rights Museum opens at 9:00 a.m. I'd like to check it out for an hour or two before we head to Nashville."

Adele sits up and stretches her arms over her head. "I want to spend as much time as possible at the Country Music Hall of Fame. I've always wanted to get my picture taken next to those Gold and Platinum record walls."

"I have to admit, I'm mostly looking forward to the costumes," I say, rummaging through my bag for some clean clothes. "They have an amazing collection of country western fashion—everything from Taylor Swift outfits, all the way back to Hillbilly dungarees and straw hats. It will make for some awesome shots for my blog."

Adele swings her legs over the edge of the bed. "You're really lucky, you know that? You have such an interesting job compared to me, not to mention the flexible hours and not having to answer to an overbearing boss anymore."

"You could quit—figure out something you'd love to do and start moving in that direction."

Adele twists her lips. "It's not that easy. You have Clay's career to fall back on if your fashion blog ever falters. And now you have an inheritance too." She gestures around the room with a flick of her wrist. "Look at this place! Neither of us could afford to stay here on my administrative salary or even your fashion blog earnings."

"I've been incredibly lucky," I admit, "But that doesn't mean you have to stay in a job you hate. Let's do some brainstorming on the drive to Nashville and come up with a few ideas. There are always other options." I toss a pillow at her. "Come on, let's grab some breakfast, and get out of here."

After feasting on a stack of fluffy, blueberry buttermilk pancakes downstairs in the Capriccio Grill, we load up the Tahoe to drive the short distance to the Civil Rights Museum.

"All right, Tour Guide Extraordinaire," I say, starting up the engine. "Feed me some facts."

"Hmm ... it says here the mission of the museum is to share the culture and lessons from the American Civil Rights Movement. It's located at the former Lorraine Motel, where civil rights leader Dr. Martin Luther King Jr. was assassinated—"

"On April fourth, nineteen sixty-eight," I cut in.

Adele flashes me a startled look. "When did you become such a history buff?"

"I'm not. I sucked at it in high school, as you very well know. But I did do some reading when I was planning out our stops. I'm determined to visit every last museum on our list and educate myself and be inspired in the process."

"I'm not sure we'll have time to do the Civil Rights Museum and the Country Music Hall of Fame in one day," Adele muses. "Nashville's a three-hour-drive from here."

"Let's just take our time, have lunch, then drive to Nashville," I say. "We can check out the live music scene there tonight, and then spend the whole next day basking in country music heaven."

Adele turns to me, her eyes sparkling. "For real? You won't get bored?"

"I'll find ways to entertain myself," I assure her, laughing at her enthusiasm. "I know you're dying to see it, so I'm happy to take our time and enjoy it. Once we get to Nashville, it's only a two-day drive to Katonah after that, so we're doing good on time."

Adele throws me a probing look. "Are you excited to see the house?"

I give an awkward shrug, not wanting to come across as ungrateful after our conversation earlier about my good fortune. "More like curious. To be honest, I'm more interested in listing it ASAP. It's not like I had a relationship with my grandmother, so there's nothing of any meaning there to me—no photos of us together, or memories of visits, or anything like that. I hate to sound so mercenary, but it really is just about collecting the money." I huff out a sigh. "Believe me, I wish it wasn't that way. I'd trade the house for the memories in a heartbeat. But she made her choice, and what's done is done."

Moments later, I pull into the museum parking lot and throw a cautious glance around at our surroundings as I reach for my purse.

"Looking for CJ?" Adele asks.

I give a reluctant nod. "We can't ignore the possibility that he's still following us."

Adele lets out a disgruntled humph. "He's wasting his time. He won't find Gianna by trailing us around museums from one city to the next." She glances at her phone. "Do you mind if we look for a drugstore before we go in? I've got a splitting headache."

I check to make sure the car is securely locked before accompanying her to a nearby Walgreens.

"I'm going to browse the make up while you get your Advil," I say.

"Sounds good. I'll come find you in a few minutes," Adele replies, before making a beeline to the pain relief aisle at the back of the store.

I wander up and down the cosmetic aisles and soon lose myself in a swathe of products. I'm trying to decide between two different eyeshadow palettes when Adele suddenly appears at my side. She clutches my arm, a look of urgency in her eyes.

"I just saw Gianna!" she blurts out.

"What?" I gasp, dropping one of the palettes to the floor. I kneel down and pick it up, staring in dismay at the cracked cover.

"Sorry," I mouth to a young sales assistant stacking a shelf nearby.

"Just toss it on the cart," she drawls, chewing gum as she continues unpacking a box of hand creams.

I turn my attention back to Adele. "Where is she?" I ask in a sharp whisper.

"Outside. She's gone now. I was standing in line to pay, and I glimpsed her through the window. She was walking down the street holding hands with some guy—it wasn't CJ."

My mouth drops open as I digest the information. Shock quickly gives way to anger. What does Gianna think she's playing at—leaving everyone hanging like that? I'd like to wring her neck, if I could get my hands on her. "Are you sure it was her?" I ask, placing the damaged eyeshadow palette on the inventory cart.

"Positive. She had her black backpack with her."

"Why didn't you go after her?"

"I tried to. I was stuck in a line of twenty people zigzagging back-and-forth between the shelving. By the time I got out of there, she'd disappeared."

I shake my head in disbelief. "It looks like she's still making her way east to Nashville. I can't believe she dumped us to hitch a ride with some guy. Why didn't she just tell us?"

Adele shrugs. "That's her business. At least now we can quit worrying about her."

I nod thoughtfully. "I need to let Officer Myers know."

Adele frowns. "Why bother? She's safe, that's good enough for me."

"I promised him I'd call if she turned up or contacted us. It's the least I can do to put her father's mind at rest." I lock eyes with Adele. "The good thing is, we're free to enjoy the rest of our trip without that cloud of worry hanging over us anymore."

"About time," Adele responds, with a pout. "I never want to hear her name again."

I fish in my purse for Officer Myer's card and place the call. It rings several times and then goes straight to voice-mail. I leave a brief message explaining the situation and give him our location. "Done!" I say, with a flourish. "Let's head to the museum."

Outside, we take a selfie by the famous Lorraine Motel sign, and then pause, for a moment, beneath the balcony where Dr. Martin Luther King Jr died. The exterior of the motel has been preserved as it was back in 1968, with the same pale turquoise paint coating the doors and net curtains covering the windows.

"That was his room where the wreath's hanging—306," Adele says, looking up at the balcony.

An unexpected weight of sadness settles over me. "It's

humbling to think of all the people who've paid the ultimate price to secure freedom. I take so much for granted."

Inside the museum, the tour begins in an exhibit hall documenting the slave trade. We file past a plaster cast replica of an auctioneer selling off a young woman and her newborn baby, and a group of half-naked slaves tied together below deck on an infamous slave ship. Even the floor is an integral part of the exhibit, designed as a map to show all the trade routes between countries across the world.

"I don't know how those slave traders were able to live with themselves," I comment to Adele.

"Look!" she says, pointing up ahead. "There's a replica of the Rosa Parks bus!"

We climb aboard to find a bronze figure of Rosa Parks sitting alone in a seat toward the front. The expression on her face is one of deep reflection, as though she knew what she was doing might cost her her freedom, or even her life, but that this was her road to walk. "You can't help but admire her courage and conviction," I say.

"I guess you have to want something badly enough to be prepared to die for it," Adele responds in a slightly wistful tone.

I throw her a sympathetic glance, guessing she's thinking about the cost of quitting her job and starting down a new path. I give her a playful nudge in the ribs. "I knew the museums would be inspiring. When you go back home, just channel Rosa Parks and march right into your boss's office, resignation letter in hand."

Toward the end of the tour, we walk past a glass wall enclosing the actual room where Dr. King spent the last night of his life. We press our foreheads against the glass and survey the contents. An ashtray full of cigarette butts sits alongside a coffee cup atop a small table near the unmade bed—evidence of a life brought to an abrupt end.

I press a button on the wall to listen to a recording of a line from Dr. King's last speech.

"That was a bit eerie," Adele says. "It almost sounded like he was predicting his own death."

A shiver runs through me. I'm not sure how much credence I give to prediction, but it brings the ominous words in Gianna's journal to mind. Against all odds, she's made it to Memphis alive. Adele almost didn't. Am I next on CJ's hit list?

We exit the building to move to the second half of the museum comprising the boarding house that James Earl Ray used as a sniper's perch to assassinate Dr. King. I'm about to step inside when my phone rings. I glance at the screen, intending to silence the call, when I notice it's an Albuquerque area code. "I have to take this," I say to Adele. "It could be Officer Myers."

She nods. "I'm going to find a bathroom. Be right back."

I slide my finger across the screen. "Cora speaking," I say, stepping aside to let other people go by.

"It's Officer Myers returning your call."

"Thanks for getting back with me," I say, tumbling over my words. "Did you listen to my message, yet? Adele saw Gianna. She's safe—she's here in Memphis!"

"I'm afraid that's not possible." Officer Myers clears his throat. "Gianna Halstead's body was discovered last night in Albuquerque."

18

I grip the phone tighter in my fist. I must have misunderstood what Officer Myers said. Gianna can't be dead—Adele just saw her. She's not in Albuquerque anymore. She's here in Memphis.

"Her body was found behind a dumpster less than a mile from the Comfort Inn you were staying at," Officer Myers continues.

I stare blankly at the steady trickle of visitors moving in and out through the museum door. Everything seems to be happening in slow motion around me. My head is swirling, and I sink down on a nearby bench, afraid I might collapse from shock. "Are you sure?" I rasp. "How do you know it's her?"

"Her father flew in today and identified her body," Officer Myers replies. "I realize this must be a shock to you. I know you were concerned about her."

"I don't understand," I say. "Adele was sure it was Gianna she saw this morning. She even had the same backpack with her."

"It must have been someone who looked like her,"

Officer Myers answers, his tone softening. "It's understand-able how Adele could have mistaken someone else for her. You said you only spent a couple of days with Gianna, after all."

"How ... how did she die?" I ask, biting down on my lip as I wait for his answer. I don't want to hear that she was murdered, but I don't want to hear that she committed suicide either—that would mean there might have been something I could have done to help her, if I hadn't been so busy judging her.

"I'm not at liberty to discuss the details of an ongoing investigation," Officer Myers answers, his tone switching back to its official crispness. "But you should be prepared for the eventuality that we'll require a statement from you and Adele. We need to find out everything we can about Gian-na's last movements in her final days. We're also trying to locate her boyfriend, CJ Phillips, to find out exactly what went down between them before she stowed away in your car."

I suck in a sharp breath at the mention of CJ. The right thing to do would be to tell Officer Myers that CJ's here in Memphis too, but I can't help thinking about his threat. Things could get complicated if suspicion falls on us. We could wind up having to hire lawyers to defend ourselves. I have a sudden vision of pouring my entire inheritance into proving our innocence.

"A detective will be in touch with you," Officer Myers adds. "Let me know right away if you hear from CJ, or if you think of anything else that might be helpful."

"Of course," I stammer.

He thanks me and hangs up. I press my shaking knees together as I try to come to terms with the news of Gianna's death. I can scarcely believe that the young, complicated, dark-haired woman riding in the back seat of my car only a few short days ago is dead. My stomach churns. It seems morbidly ironic that I've been given the news about Gianna here and now, outside the boarding house where a fateful shot ended Dr. King's life.

"I'm back!" Adele says, bouncing up to me. "What are you looking so gloomy about?"

I hold her gaze, trying to find the words to break it to her. She was so relieved earlier when she told me she'd seen Gianna. We really dared to hope that the rest of our trip would be smooth sailing. "That wasn't Gianna you saw outside Walgreens," I say hesitantly. "Officer Myers just called me. Her body was discovered at the back of a dumpster near our hotel in Albuquerque."

Adele takes a half step backward, blinking in confusion. "What? That's not possible. How do they know it's her?"

"Her father identified her body."

Adele's lips open and close like a blowfish as she digests the shocking news. "I knew that was CJ's camper following us on the highway. Gianna was right that it was only a matter of time before he found her." Her brow wrinkles. "Maybe she agreed to meet him that morning and they had an argument or something, and he killed her." Her voice trails off. "I just can't take it in. She was sleeping in our hotel room only a couple of nights ago."

I lean over and let my head sink into my hands. "It's awful. I can't process it."

A passing staff member with a dangling lanyard walks up to me, frowning. "Ma'am, are you all right?"

"She's fine, thanks," Adele replies on my behalf. "She just needs a little fresh air."

"I have to get out of here," I say, abruptly getting to my feet.

Adele gestures to the second half of the museum. "Sure you don't want to see the boarding house?"

"I can't stomach any more," I reply. "I just want to get on the road and check into our hotel in Nashville and lay my head on a pillow.

Adele nods. "Is it my turn to drive?"

I give a helpless shrug. "I've lost track, but if you want to, I won't say no. I'm pretty gutted right now—not sure I can concentrate enough to drive."

I barely make it back to the car before my legs give out beneath me. Sinking down in the passenger seat, I close my eyes, snippets of conversations with Gianna coming to mind.

I think he killed his last girlfriend. He'll find me. I know he will. The desert's a great place to hide a body.

I'm overcome with guilt at how much I distrusted her story of abuse—even suspecting her of trying to scam us at one point. I try to picture what I could have done differently to stop this from happening. I thought I was keeping her safe by letting her travel with us. As it turns out, all my efforts were in vain. One wrong exit led to murder.

Adele shoots me a concerned look. "Are you okay?"

"Not really." I open my eyes and stare through the windscreen at nothing in particular. "The police need our statements."

"Why? We already told them everything we know."

"Yeah, but that was when Gianna went missing," I remind her. "It's different now that she's dead. Officer Myers wouldn't tell me how she died, but it's pretty obvious they suspect she was murdered—they're trying to track down CJ."

"Did you tell the police he's in Memphis?" Adele asks warily.

"Not yet." I bite down on my lip. "But we're going to have to report the assault now. If he killed Gianna, he needs to be brought to justice." I fix a beseeching gaze on Adele. "He held a gun to your stomach. That's proof of how violent and aggressive he is toward women. The cops need to be able to build a case against him to secure a conviction. You can help with that. CJ's a vile person—don't forget what Gianna said about his previous girlfriend going missing too. Who knows how many other women he's assaulted or killed?"

Adele's shoulders tighten, her hands clamped to the steering wheel.

I sigh and try again. "Look, I know you're scared of him, but the police will find him and arrest him, sooner rather than later, if we let them know where he is."

"*Was*," Adele corrects me. "We don't know if he's still in Memphis."

"Maybe not, but the longer we stay silent, the more time we're giving him to disappear."

Adele's phone begins to ring from the depths of her purse.

"Want me to get that?" I ask, reaching behind her seat.

"No," she says wearily. "It's probably my parents wanting to complain about Jackson again. I can't deal with them right now, not on top of all this."

"I can ask Clay to talk to Jackson, if you like," I offer, secretly hoping she won't take me up on it. The last thing I need is to get into another argument with Clay about Adele's dysfunctional family.

"That won't help. Trust me, Jackson doesn't listen to anyone," Adele replies. "I appreciate the offer, but there's no sense in getting Clay involved."

We fall silent for several miles, neither of us in the mood

for our Pollyannish karaoke playlist. I'm starting to nod off when Adele mutters something under her breath.

"Hmm?" I say, sliding up in my seat and blinking myself awake.

"There's a camper truck behind us," Adele mutters through gritted teeth.

I swivel around in my seat, adrenalin suddenly overpowering the sleepiness in my veins. My breath comes in short, sharp stabs as my eyes frantically scan the traffic. "Where?"

"Behind that Freightliner car hauler. You'll be able to see it when we go around this next bend."

Moments later, I spot a beat-up white camper truck that looks all too familiar. My heart shudders in my chest. I'm almost certain it's CJ's camper.

"Is it him?" Adele asks, her voice rising in panic. "I thought his truck was gray, but maybe you were right." I can tell she's flustered because her driving is becoming more erratic by the minute—braking and accelerating as she tries to outsmart the flow of traffic and pull ahead. Her eyes keep swiveling back to the rearview mirror like magnets. "He said we hadn't heard the last from him," she mutters. "What if he follows us all the way to Nashville? He might think we're taking Gianna to her parents."

"I'm calling Officer Myers," I say, pulling out my phone. "CJ can't touch us if he's in custody."

"What if he tells the police we murdered Gianna?" Adele asks, swerving into the fast lane. "I'm scared of what could happen."

A horn blares behind us, and Adele quickly accelerates and searches for an opening to get back into the slow lane.

"Quit all the passing!" I cry. "You're not going to get away from him like this—you're just going to wreck. I'm calling the police right now."

Adele maneuvers back into the slow lane, her lips set in a grim line.

Thankfully, Officer Myers answers his phone on the first ring.

"It's Cora Lewis," I say. "CJ's following us. He's in an Arctic Fox white camper truck heading east on the I-40."

"What's your location?" Officer Myers asks.

"We're about an hour out of Memphis on our way to Nashville. We just passed the sign for the Tina Turner Museum, about five minutes ago."

"I'll notify local law enforcement and have them pull him over."

"Will you let us know if it's him?" I ask.

"Absolutely," Officer Myers confirms. "Stay on the highway until you hear from me. Do you have enough gas to keep driving?"

"For now. We'll need to gas up again before we get to Nashville."

"We'll intercept him before that."

I hang up and drop the phone in my lap. "He's dispatching highway patrol to pull him over. Hopefully, they arrest him on the spot for murder."

Adele remains rigid in her seat, her fingers restlessly gripping and releasing the steering wheel. "I just don't understand how he always knows where we are."

A tingling sensation creeps across the back of my neck as the truth dawns on me. I turn to face her. "CJ must have been tracking us this whole time."

Her face pales. "How?"

"Most likely a tracking device on the car. Maybe Gianna installed it."

Adele throws me a horrified look. "How do we find it?

Don't those Apple air tags notify your phone if they're being used nearby?"

"I think so, but there's a ton of different tracking devices you can put on cars these days."

Adele glances in the rearview mirror. "He's still there. He's making sure to stay several vehicles behind us, but he's not letting us out of his sight."

"I told you his truck was white," I say.

"We don't know for sure that it's him," Adele replies. "It might not—" She breaks off mid-sentence, eyes widening.

I swing around in my seat to see what's caught her attention.

Relief floods through me at the welcome sight of flashing blue and red lights.

19

I watch as the white camper truck brakes and pulls over onto the shoulder, spewing a cloud of dust into the lane of traffic. "They've got him," I exclaim. "It's over."

"Not until we know for sure it's CJ," Adele says grimly.

Despite being adamant about not wanting to celebrate prematurely, her grip on the steering wheel visibly relaxes. The relief of knowing that CJ can't hurt us anymore has to be especially poignant for Adele. She knows all too well the terrifying reality of what it means to be at his mercy.

Twenty minutes later, I get a call from Officer Myers. "I'm happy to inform you that CJ Phillips has been detained by the Tennessee Highway Patrol and taken in for questioning."

"*It was him*," I mouth to Adele.

"You're safe, for now," Officer Myers adds.

For now sounds slightly ominous, a backhanded warning of sorts that they won't be able to hold CJ for long. The police still haven't divulged how Gianna died. They're probably waiting on the autopsy results. If it's ruled a suicide, they'll only be able to detain CJ long enough to ask him about Gianna's state of mind and movements in her last days. But, if the evidence shows she was murdered, he'll most definitely be a person of interest.

"I appreciate your assistance in apprehending him," Officer Myers goes on. "Someone from the Tennessee police department will follow up with you."

After thanking him, I end the call and drop my phone into the console. "That's it, it's finally over," I say, releasing a sigh.

Adele gives a dubious shake of her head. "Maybe not. If CJ didn't kill Gianna, he's going to be as shocked as we were when he learns they've found her body."

"At least he'll know now we weren't hiding her from him. He won't have any reason to come after us anymore."

"But he'll know it was us who called the police on him," Adele responds in a tremulous tone. "If they don't have enough evidence to hold him for murder, they'll have to release him. We could be in more danger now than ever."

I let the stark reality of Adele's words sink in. For a few short moments, I allowed myself to imagine the remainder of our trip could proceed free of the ominous threat of CJ hanging over it. The truth is, the minute he's released from police custody, he'll come after us like a venomous snake we've provoked. "We'll just have to stay alert and be smart about safety," I say. "If CJ can't find us, he can't harm us. As soon as we get to Nashville, we'll search the Tahoe for that tracking device."

"He has your phone number too," Adele points out.

"I'll block him," I say. "It won't help him find us anyway."

"How long do you think they'll detain him for—a couple of hours, or days?"

"It depends on whether Gianna was murdered, and if he's a suspect." I fix an earnest gaze on Adele. "You know we could get him locked up if you'd agree to press charges. He assaulted you with a deadly weapon. That's a serious crime. It's not just your word against his. I was there too—I witnessed everything."

"No!" Adele says sharply. "If he makes good on his threat and convinces the police that we did something to Gianna, we could end up embroiled in a murder investigation. I could lose my job over it. I'd never forgive myself if I wasn't available to help my parents because I was too busy trying to avoid serving time in prison. It would be enough to kill them. It's bad enough that Jackson's in and out of juvenile hall."

"That's not going to happen," I say, with an inflated level of conviction.

"You don't know that. Gianna said CJ was a very convincing liar," Adele counters. "It doesn't matter that we're innocent. We could spend years of our lives, and all your money, defending ourselves. It happens all the time. Think about it. If CJ has an alibi for Gianna's murder, then we're the only other suspects." She sets her lips in a thin line. "You've dragged us into the middle of this mess whether you wanted to or not."

I throw her an injured look. "I said I was sorry. How was I supposed to know things would turn out this way?"

"If you'd listen to the people in your life more often, we wouldn't be in this predicament. You're so stubborn when you fixate on something."

I toss my head in annoyance. It's unfair of Adele to lay all the blame at my feet. We both agreed that if Gianna's story checked out, we'd give her a ride to Nashville. We covered all our bases and took all the right cautionary steps. We searched her backpack, and even made her call her parents to verify her story. "I couldn't abandon an abused woman with no money, and no phone, who had the courage to hide in a stranger's car to escape her violent boyfriend," I say. "And, by the way, the violent boyfriend part of her story checked out, as you found out for yourself when he jammed a gun into your stomach."

"It would never have happened, if you'd listened to me in the first place," Adele yells. "I'm lucky to be alive!"

I fold my arms and glower out the side window. I hate arguing with Adele. I feel guilty enough already about putting her life in danger without her rubbing it in. Clay would agree wholeheartedly with everything she said. He'd accuse me of being reckless and selfish, when all I was trying to do was extend a little compassion to a frightened young woman.

I turn on the audiobook I'm only halfway invested in to mask the awkward silence that fills the car like a damp fog.

By the time we stop to gas up, the tension between Adele and me has simmered its way down to nothing.

"I'm sorry—" Adele begins.

"No!" I cut her off. "You've got nothing to be sorry about. You're right. I made a stupid call. I should have stuck to my guns and dropped Gianna off at a shelter or given her some money so she could get to wherever she needed to go. It was a dumb decision on my part to cave to her request. I wish I could go back and change things. I talked this whole trip up and convinced you to come, and now I've gone and ruined everything."

Adele shrugs. "You're being too hard on yourself. I know it wasn't intentional. Besides, the trip's not completely ruined. We've still got the Country Music Hall of Fame to look forward to."

I flash her a rueful grin. "Let's hope it lives up to its reputation and makes this all worthwhile. I'll start looking for a hotel once we get back on the road."

"Speaking of getting back on the road, I can scarcely see through this window anymore." Adele grabs a squeegee and starts cleaning off the bugs splattered across the windscreen.

I reach for the nozzle to fill the tank, relieved we've cleared the air between us.

An hour later, we pull into the parking lot of the Best Western located in downtown Nashville. Adele turns to me, a familiar sparkle back in her eyes. "I can't believe we're finally here! What do you say we check out Broadway Street and catch some live music?"

"Sounds like a plan," I reply. "First, we need to tear the Tahoe apart and find that tracker."

Adele's face clouds over. "I'd forgotten all about it."

"Let's start by looking under the car," I suggest. "That's the most likely place to hide something."

We switch on the flashlights on our phones and get down on our knees to peer into the dirty nooks and crannies on the underside of the car.

"We should have gone through a car wash before we attempted this," I groan. "We're going to look a hot mess checking in to the hotel."

A gray-haired man in a suit and tie walks by, swinging a briefcase. He breaks his stride when he sees us and does a quick assessment of the situation. "Everything all right?" he calls to us. "Do you have a flat?"

"No! We're fine, thanks," I reply, laughing self-consciously. "Just uh ... dropped something."

The man gives a curt nod and continues walking down the ramp, satisfied he's done his duty without obligating himself to get down on his knees in his suit.

"I don't even know what I'm looking for," Adele says, waving her phone haphazardly back-and-forth like a searchlight under the car.

"Anything that looks like it doesn't belong," I answer, running my hands along the underside of the frame. "A small magnetic box, or something similar, attached to the metal part of the car."

Adele frowns. "It's kind of hard to know what parts are detachable. I've never actually looked beneath a car before."

"Neither have I," I admit, my mind going back to Clay's snub when he was trying to talk me out of this trip. *You can't even change a flat.* Little did he know that I'd be facing greater challenges than a flat tire. Nothing could have prepared me for anything like this.

"Ugh, my legs are killing me," Adele says, straightening up. "I don't see anything."

"Let's try under the hood," I suggest.

"How could CJ open the hood without a key?"

"Good point," I say, struggling to my feet. "Still, better safe than sorry. He might have managed to slip a tracker in at the gas station in Barstow while we were occupied with that old man. We left the car unlocked."

"Maybe," Adele responds, sounding unconvinced.

I pop the lid and we stand, side-by-side, staring down at the engine.

"See anything unusual?" I ask.

"Yeah, all of it," Adele replies, raising her brows in dramatic fashion.

I chuckle as I poke around in the engine compartment, looking for any type of removable device. "Ouch!" I yell, yanking my fingers back. "The engine's still hot."

"We're wasting our time. There's nothing here," Adele says. "I bet you can't even put a tracking device in an engine compartment. Wouldn't it melt?"

I shrug as I slam the lid closed. "There's only one other possibility—Gianna might have put a tracker inside the car."

We open all the car doors and get to work searching the door pockets, under the mats, and behind the seats.

"I found some of her trash," Adele says, gingerly holding up a scrunched-up coffee cup and a Snickers candy bar wrapper between two fingers.

"Let's take all our belongings out," I say. "She was hiding under our stuff for several hours so she might have stashed the tracker in the back somewhere."

Adele groans. "Do we have to take out *everything*?"

"Only if you want to be safe," I answer, reprovingly.

We spend the next few minutes unloading our belongings and combing every inch of the rear of the Tahoe. I even open the small compartment containing the jack and survey the contents dubiously. "I'm pretty sure that's just the jack in there."

"I say we pack it in," Adele groans, stifling a yawn. "This is a waste of time."

I shake out our sleeping bags for good measure, and then begin loading all our gear back into the car. "If either Gianna or CJ installed a tracker, they did a good job of hiding it," I say, with a defeated sigh.

Adele frowns. "I wonder if CJ removed it in Memphis."

I trace my fingers lightly across my brow, considering the possibility. "If that's the case, how did he end up behind us on the I-40 again?"

"He could have simply waited for us to leave the museum parking lot and followed us."

I grimace as I lock the car and reach for my wheeled bag. "Devious as well as dangerous—at least he's in police custody, for now."

After brushing ourselves off as best we can, we make our way inside the Best Western to check in.

"I've got dibs on the shower first," I say, as soon as we get to our room.

"Five minutes," Adele replies, yanking her suitcase around the door. "I want to spend as much time as possible soaking up the Nashville nightlife."

After cleaning up, we reconvene to critique each other's outfits—eventually settling on western shirts and bootcut jeans.

"Ready for some honky-tonk?" Adele asks, putting the final touches on her makeup.

"Food's the first thing on my agenda," I reply.

We don our cowboy hats and hit the street to walk the two blocks to Broadway.

"What sounds good to you?" Adele asks.

"Some of Nashville's famous fried chicken." I pull out my phone to check our options. "There's a chicken shack on Broadway that has great reviews."

"Lead the way," Adele says, grinning at me from beneath the rim of her cowboy hat. "Hopefully, we don't get blisters from our new boots."

Music blasts at us from every other doorway along the way to Hattie B's hot chicken shack. Inside, we manage to snag a small table at the back.

"I have to admit, this is finger-licking good," I say, with a contented sigh, as I reach into my red-and-white-checkered carton for another piece of spicy fried chicken. "I'm stuffed, but there's no way I'm leaving this."

"Jackson would love the pimento mac and cheese," Adele says, dipping her plastic spoon into a cardboard carton. "It's his favorite."

"Did you ever call your parents back?" I ask, wiping my sticky fingers on a napkin.

A flicker of consternation crosses Adele's face. "No, I

forgot. I'm not going to do it now with all this racket. I'll wait until I get back to the hotel. It can't have been important or they would have tried calling me again by now."

I reach for one last crinkle cut fry, even though I'll have to loosen my belt a notch to move. "Ready to walk around town for a bit?" I say.

"Yeah, sure. I'm just going to run to the restroom first," Adele replies.

I tidy up our mess and carry the trash over to a nearby station. While I wait for Adele to return, I check my phone, but there are no new messages from Clay. I send him a quick text letting him know we made it to Nashville safely and that I'll call him tomorrow. After responding to several new comments on my social media postings, I slip my phone back into my purse and make my way to the restroom to check on Adele.

As I push open the door, I hear her voice, high-pitched and angry. "Well, you should care! I could have been killed."

20

_____

Without a word, I let the heavy bathroom door close behind me and hurry back to our table to wait for Adele to return. I'm guessing she decided to call her parents back, after all. It sounds as though she might have told them about the assault—which shocks me. Maybe she was counting on an outpouring of concern, although it didn't seem like she got the reaction she was hoping for. I know she feels overlooked and under-appreciated by them—which is another reason I thought this trip away would be good for her.

Five more minutes go by, before I spot her making her way back through the restaurant to our table.

"Sorry I took so long," she says, sounding flustered as she sinks down in her chair.

"Food not agreeing with you?" I quip, not wanting to pressure her into telling me about her argument.

She eyes me with a questioning air. "Was that you who peeked around the bathroom door and beat a hasty retreat?"

I give an abashed shrug. "I didn't want to intrude. Figured it was your parents you were on the phone with."

She sighs. "I shouldn't have got so worked up and yelled at them. Sorry you had to hear that."

I give her a sympathetic smile. "I didn't hear much—just that you could have been killed." I twist my hands in my lap. "Did you tell them about the assault?"

Adele's shoulders sag. "I shouldn't have bothered. They're more worried about some video game Jackson's playing at all hours of the night at his friend's house. Somehow, a stranger pulling a gun on me in a parking lot isn't enough to evoke their concern. Don't worry, I didn't go into details about Gianna."

"I'm sorry," I say. "That really sucks." My heart breaks for her, and I feel angry with her parents, at the same time. For once, it would be nice if they showed her that they cared. It seems as if they only use her as a resource officer for Jackson, and they've forgotten that she's their child too. I can't blame Adele for trying to help. If it were my brother, I would do the same. At the end of the day, family is all any of us have. Maybe that's why I'm so eager to start one of my own with Clay—I have no one else left in my life.

"They even asked me to fly home. They're at their wit's end. I told them that's not going to happen. Anyway, enough about my dysfunctional family," Adele says, slapping her palms on the table. "Let's get out of here. It's honky-tonk time."

We wander out onto the sidewalk thronged with people and saunter along Broadway, stopping in neon-lit doorways to listen to the various live bands as we pass by. Out on the street, a steady stream of themed, open-top buses transport exuberant bachelorette parties around the city. Young women in cowboy hats clutch their alcoholic beverages of choice as they sway their hips to the incessant country beat pumping out from the buses. They wave at everyone as they pass by—clearly enjoying the attention their immoderately tanned legs in denim cutoff shorts are garnering.

"This place is cowboy crazy!" Adele shouts to me over the mayhem. "I love it!"

I smile as her infectious excitement spills over me like a refreshing shower. This is the old Adele I've known since childhood—bubbly, and full of spunk and optimism. I know I've neglected her since Clay and I got married, but it's only now we're taking this trip together that I realize how much I've missed having her in my life. In a burst of spontaneity, I grab her by the waist and start a clumsy two-step to the music. "No time like the present to break in our boots," I shout.

She laughs, and joins in, attempting, and failing miserably, to keep time with the beat pulsing out from a nearby pub.

My phone buzzes in my pocket and I break away from Adele to fish it out. I groan inwardly when I see that it's Clay —I already told him we were heading out and that I'd call him tomorrow. I stare at the screen for a moment, wondering whether to ignore it.

"Is it the police?" Adele pants in my ear, breathless from our two-stepping down the street.

"What?" I frown at her in confusion.

"You said the Tennessee police would be following up with us," she says impatiently.

"Oh yeah. No, it's just Clay." I let the call go to voicemail and then slip the phone back into my pocket. "I'll call him back later. I won't be able to hear him out here."

Adele links an arm through mine and we walk on, squeezing past a small group of people gathered around a street musician.

"Don't you think it's kind of odd the police haven't contacted us yet?" Adele yells in my ear.

I shrug. "Not really. I'm sure they've got their hands full with more important things than taking our statements. What are we going to tell them that they don't already know?"

"That CJ's been stalking us since Barstow, for starters."

I raise my brows at her. "It's hardly their chief concern. They're more interested in the possibility that he murdered Gianna—maybe his previous girlfriend too."

Adele grimaces. "We could have been next on his hit list. I mean he—"

She breaks off when my phone starts buzzing. I pull it out and roll my eyes. "It's Clay, *again*. I don't know what his problem is."

"Maybe you should answer it," Adele says. "We can look for somewhere quiet so you can talk."

I shake my head. "I'm just going to wait until we get back to the hotel. I'll have to update him about Gianna, and CJ's arrest. He'll have a million questions, and I don't want to get into it with him out here. Let's keep walking."

Outside a Western supply store, we stop to take a selfie next to a life-sized boot.

"Smile, cowgirl!" Adele says, holding her phone out at arm's length as we strike a pose, hands on our hips. As she presses the shutter, her phone beeps with an incoming text. She glances at it and throws me a strange look. "It's your hubby. He wants you to call him."

"I can't believe this," I huff in frustration.

"Why don't we just head back to the hotel now?" Adele suggests. "We got a little taste of the nightlife already, and you got a few good pics for your blog."

I give a reluctant nod. I can't put off the inevitable

conversation with Clay forever. It's time I told him what happened to Gianna.

We walk the two blocks back to our hotel, the beat coming from Broadway growing ever fainter behind us. Back in our room, I pull off my boots and stretch out on my bed to call Clay back. I press the speaker button and toss the phone onto the pillow next to me.

"Finally! I've been trying to call you," he explodes, before I have a chance to say a word.

"I told you we were going out," I reply. "I couldn't pick up —there was music blasting out of every doorway. Adele and I could barely hear each other speak."

"Are there any updates with the situation?" Clay asks.

Adele throws me a pitying look before returning her attention to her own phone.

"They found Gianna. She's dead," I say flatly.

"Dead?" Clay exclaims. "How do you know she's dead?"

"The police found her body by a dumpster near the hotel we were staying at in Albuquerque."

After a heartbeat of silence, Clay asks, "Do they know what happened to her?"

"They're not saying, but I'm guessing by the way they're handling it that it wasn't an accident or suicide." I pick at the skin on my thumb. "CJ followed us to Nashville. We alerted the police and they detained him on the highway. They took him in for questioning."

Clay sucks in a sharp breath. "They arrested him?"

"I'm not sure. They might have just detained him. The police didn't tell us much—they're supposed to contact us to take our statements, so we'll find out more then."

"Cora, listen to me," Clay says, his voice low and urgent. "You're in serious danger. You need to abandon this trip and come home at once."

"I'm not turning around now," I protest. "CJ's in custody."

"For how long? He could be out in a matter of hours." Clay's voice rises. "Gianna's dead. What makes you think you won't be next?"

I shoot a worried look at Adele who has abandoned feigning interest in her Instagram feed and is staring at me, eyes wide with fear. I need to end this conversation before she has second thoughts about traveling any further with me. "We don't know for sure that Gianna was murdered," I say. "Maybe she'd had enough of CJ's abuse and decided that taking her own life was the best option to end the pain."

"You don't actually believe that!" Clay snaps. "The police wouldn't have hauled CJ off in a squad car if Gianna had killed herself."

I think back to the flashing lights of the two highway patrol vehicles that pulled over CJ's camper truck. I have to agree with Clay. The Tennessee sheriffs would have handled things with a lot more discretion if they'd been tasked with telling CJ his girlfriend had committed suicide.

"You don't know if the police have any evidence against CJ," Clay rambles on. "What if he comes after you again as soon as he's released?"

"He's not going to do anything stupid with the police breathing down his neck," I say.

"He might! He's obviously crazy. You could be in serious danger. I'm booking a flight to Nashville," Clay announces. "You can pick me up at the airport tomorrow and we'll drive the rest of the way together."

"Don't be ridiculous," I protest. "Adele and I are handling the situation."

"How's that going so far? You picked up a hitchhiker who turns up dead, and now her violent boyfriend is stalking you!" Clay yells. "It's not up for discussion. I'll postpone my exam."

"What about work? It's tax season."

"I'll quit if I have to."

I glance across at Adele and give a helpless shrug. I'm not sure how she's going to react to Clay gatecrashing our trip.

She flaps a hand dismissively at me. "*Let him come*," she mouths.

I frown and look back down at my phone lying on the pillow next to me. Maybe it would ease Adele's fears if Clay was with us. His presence might even be enough to deter CJ from attempting to make good on his threat. Besides, it's not as if Clay can't find a new job now that we'll have my inheritance to tide us over. "Okay," I say with a resigned sigh. "Text me your flight details and we'll pick you up."

"I'll jump right on it," Clay says, sounding relieved. "Are you still planning on going to the Country Music Hall of Fame tomorrow?"

"Absolutely!" I say, grinning across at Adele.

"Good, you should be safe in crowded places," Clay replies. "Stay away from deserted parking lots and the like. You can't count on the police to inform you in a timely manner that CJ is back out on the street."

"We'll be fine. See you tomorrow." I hang up and fall back among the pillows. "I'm so sorry, Adele. It looks like we've just acquired another unsolicited passenger."

She shrugs and flashes me a wan smile. "Better one we know than a stranger."

21

The following morning, Adele and I check out of our hotel and stroll out to the Tahoe, pumped up about our upcoming visit to the Country Music Hall of Fame. Adele appears more relaxed, and isn't peering nervously over her shoulder like she's been doing ever since the assault. I think she's relieved to know that Clay is joining us today, even though it will change the dynamic in the car. Our girls' trip essentially ends this morning after our visit to the museum, but at least we're going out on a high.

"Let's clean out the car before we pick up Clay," I suggest, eyeing the empty coffee cups, napkins, and wrappers stuffed into every crevice.

Adele pulls a plastic grocery bag out from under the seat. "I'll take care of the trash," she says. "You make space for his luggage."

I get busy organizing our scattered belongings and clearing off the back seat so that Clay has somewhere to sit. I feel kind of weird putting him in Gianna's seat, which is silly of me—it's not as if she died there. Still, there's something creepy about knowing my husband is taking a dead woman's place.

We'll need to head to the airport around 2:00 p.m. to pick him up, which gives us all morning in the museum. Clay made it clear that he wants to get on the road right away and try and make it as far as Roanoke tonight, which will leave us only one more day of driving before we reach Katonah. A tingle of excitement goes through me. It hasn't quite sunk in yet that I'm on the verge of becoming the rightful owner of a million-dollar home.

"That should do it," I say to Adele, as I close the back door of the Tahoe. "Let's get out of here."

She takes the grocery bag of trash over to the can by the hotel entrance and dumps it before climbing in.

We drive the short distance to the museum and manage to find parking in a public lot nearby.

"This is it, we're finally here!" Adele gushes, grabbing my arm and squeezing it as we walk briskly up to the main entrance. "Picture time!"

I dutifully pose by the sign outside the museum for what's bound to be the first of a zillion selfies we'll take over the course of the morning.

"Can you believe they have over two-and-a-half-million country music artifacts in here?" Adele babbles, stuffing her phone back into her purse. "It's the largest collection in the world. Everything from instruments to memorabilia, and stage outfits. Shame we can't take video inside—I want to relive this experience when we go home."

I'm not a huge country music fan, but I can't help feeding off Adele's excitement as we get in line to buy our tickets. I'm determined not to sully our time here with any mention of Gianna or CJ. We don't have as long as we'd originally thought, now that we have to pick up Clay, so I'm determined to make sure Adele has a chance to savor everything the museum has to offer. It's the least I can do after the disastrous turn our trip has taken.

Once the line of people snakes its way inside, we begin moving through the exhibition halls documenting the history of country music all the way back to its folk roots. Before long, I find myself immersed in the experience, exploring the exhibits, interactive touchscreens, and photographs with almost as much enthusiasm as Adele. "Check out that white convertible with the gun handles," I say, as we wander among glass showcases chockfull of concert paraphernalia and costumes.

"I can't believe they have the Pontiac from Smokey and the Bandit," Adele adds. "Clay's going to wish he could have got here in time to see that."

Instinctively, I throw a quick glance at my phone, but we still have plenty of time to explore. We can grab a sandwich in the museum cafe for lunch and then head to the airport. I'm nervous about how Clay's going to react when he sees me. Hopefully, he doesn't chew me out in front of Adele.

"Keith Urban sure likes black, doesn't he?" Adele observes, pointing to a display case featuring a collection of his stage costumes.

"And shirts with ruffles, apparently," I add with a laugh.

"Look!" Adele shrieks, gesturing to an exhibit up ahead. "It's my girl—Shania Twain! I adore her outfits—that pink one with the matching cowboy hat is iconic. I always wanted one just like it." She pulls out her phone and starts snapping pictures. "Her clothes are gorgeous. Thank goodness Hee Haw overalls are no longer a thing!"

"She's petite. I can't believe how tiny some of these country music stars are," I say. "Look at that gown of Faith Hill's!"

After critiquing the remainder of the outfits on display, and taking a bunch of photos for my blog, we continue our tour along several floor-to-ceiling walls filled with decades' worth of gold and platinum music awards.

"You name it, they're here!" Adele says in a hushed tone of awe. "Johnny Cash, Elvis Presley, Hank Williams, Alan Jackson, Reba McEntire, Dolly Parton, Garth Brooks."

When she's had her fill of locating and photographing all her favorite country western singers, we exit the museum and make our way to the small cafe on the terrace overlooking downtown Nashville.

"There isn't much on this menu," Adele says, glancing over it. "Snacks, mostly."

I shrug. "I'm not that hungry anyway. Let's just grab a coffee here and then we can eat after we pick up Clay."

"Did you know you have to be invited to become a member of the Country Music Hall of Fame?" Adele says, once we settle into our seats with our drinks. "It's a huge honor. Not every—"

"Cora Lewis?"

I jerk around in my seat at the authoritative voice commanding my attention, blinking in confusion as a badge is flashed in my face.

"May I?" a shrewd-eyed man says, gesturing to an empty chair.

Without waiting for a response, he sits down opposite me. He's joined by a second man I didn't notice shadowing him at first—thin, short, of Asian descent. Both are clean-shaven, dressed in dark suits with impossible-to-read expressions. My heart gallops in my chest as my brain scrambles to make sense of their presence. They must be with the Tennessee police department. I'm shocked they were able to track us down here. Perhaps they contacted

Clay and he told them where to find us. "Are you ... detectives?" I stutter.

The shrewd-eyed man's lips twitch in a cursory smile. "FBI. I'm Agent Reed."

I turn to look at Adele in time to see the color leeching from her face. She sets down her mug with a thunk, then reaches with trembling fingers for her napkin to mop up the coffee she's spilled in the process.

"This is my partner, Agent Cho," Reed continues, gesturing to the other man.

Cho inclines his head slightly, unsmiling.

"We have a few questions for you concerning Gianna Halstead," Reed says.

I squeeze my hands together in my lap. "I don't understand. I thought the police were going to follow up with us. Why is the FBI getting involved?"

Reed's expression remains blank. "Our assistance was requested. It's not unusual in a murder case that crosses state lines."

"Murder?" I echo.

"I'm afraid so. The autopsy confirmed the findings." Reed pulls out a notebook and begins flicking through it before he finds the page he's looking for. "I understand you discovered Gianna hiding in your car when you stopped in Kingman, is that correct?"

I throw Adele a harried glance. "Yes. She got in when we gassed up in Barstow."

"Did you recognize her?" Reed asks.

Adele frowns. "We thought we might have seen her in the camper truck with her boyfriend, CJ, at the gas station, but we didn't get a good look at her."

Cho leans forward, expectantly. "Did either of you know Gianna or CJ previously?"

"No," Adele and I say in unison.

"Is there any possibility Gianna might have targeted your vehicle?" Reed asks, dragging the words out as though he wants us to think the question over carefully.

I shake my head, immediately dismissing the idea. "No. It was random. An elderly man had a medical emergency, and I was distracted trying to help him. There's no way Gianna could have predicted that. She was desperate to get away from CJ. She saw her opportunity and took it."

I look to Adele for confirmation.

"Absolutely," she agrees.

Reed scribbles for a moment in his notebook.

"CJ thinks we had something to do with Gianna's disappearance," I add. "That's why he was following us. He won't get bail, will he?"

Reed pins a penetrating gaze on me. "*Did* you have something to do with her disappearance?"

I suck in a sudden breath, taken aback at the loaded question. "No! Of course not. We were only trying to help her by giving her a ride to Nashville. She ditched us without any explanation."

Reed continues to stare at me, as if waiting on me to go on.

"She used us. She even stole Adele's iPad," I add, feeling the need to underline our charitable naïveté.

Cho clears his throat before addressing Adele. "How do you know Gianna stole it?"

Adele fidgets in her seat, clearly flustered. "Because my iPad was nowhere to be found after she disappeared. What else was I supposed to think? She mentioned something about her boyfriend accusing her of stealing his phone, I figured maybe it was a pattern with her."

Cho leans back in his chair, allowing Reed to resume his line of questioning.

"Did Gianna give any indication of where she might have gone?" Reed asks.

I shrug. "The only thing she told us was that she wanted to go to Nashville—to her parents."

Reed fingers his chin thoughtfully. "Did she have any clothes with her, a bag or anything?"

"Only a black backpack," Adele answers.

"We had to stop and pick up a few toiletries and basics for her along the way," I add.

"Did she leave anything behind in your car?" Reed asks.

I balk, my wide-eyed gaze briefly locking with his. No doubt, he's an expert in recognizing when someone's lying to him. But what choice do I have? I can't bring up the journal, not without casting suspicion on Adele and me. It's not just the content that makes us look guilty—it's the fact that we didn't turn it over to the police to begin with. It's evidence, and I'm pretty sure concealing evidence is a crime of some sort. I rub my sweating palms together, avoiding stealing a glance in Adele's direction. It will only make it seem as if we're doubling down on some unspoken agreement.

"Nothing but trash," I say, with a nonchalant shrug. "She left plenty of that behind. She took her backpack with her."

Reed straightens up in his seat. "We're going to need to process your vehicle—it's standard procedure."

"What?" I ask, panic instantly welling up inside me. I rack my brains trying to remember if the FBI have a right to search my vehicle. Don't they need a warrant? But if I refuse, it's going to look like I've got something to hide. "I ... I need to pick my husband up from the airport this afternoon."

"It shouldn't take long," Reed replies, getting to his feet. "If you don't mind accompanying us to the local precinct."

I lead the way in a daze to the parking garage where we left the Tahoe. What does *process your vehicle* even mean? Are they going to tear the car apart, or do they simply want to lift Gianna's prints to make sure she was in it? My thoughts are tumbling over themselves as I run through my limited options. I could come clean about the journal before they discover it. Or I could stuff it back under the seat and feign ignorance when they find it. Maybe I could even dispose of it before we get to the station. A vision flashes before my eyes of Adele tearing out pages and throwing them out the window as we drive, like a pair of drug addicts in a desperate bid to offload evidence of illegal substances before we're apprehended.

My hopes are dashed when we get to the Tahoe and Cho holds out his hand for the key. "I'll drive your vehicle. You two can ride along with Reed."

Adele and I barely exchange a word on the way to the station. My thoughts are consumed with the horror of being accused of murder and everything that entails. On the one hand, it seems preposterous, but this morning I would have said it was laughable to think the FBI would apprehend us in the Country Music Hall of Fame.

Inside the police station, a female officer escorts us to a sparsely furnished interview room.

"Can I get you anything to drink? Coffee, water?" she offers.

I shake my head. The coffee I drank earlier is already swirling ominously in my gut.

"Coffee for me, black," Reed answers.

"How long is this going to take?" I ask. "My husband's flight gets in at 2:25 p.m."

Reed glances at his watch. "Have him catch an Uber here. Cho might need a couple of hours."

"A couple of hours!" I exclaim. "Is this really necessary? What exactly are you looking for?"

Reed stares back at me dispassionately. "Anything that shouldn't be there."

A tingling feeling spreads slowly through me as I realize what he's saying. This isn't about confirming Gianna was in my car—they're looking for evidence that she was killed in it.

22

There's no good way to explain to Clay why, at the last minute, I'm suddenly unable to pick him up at the airport.

Guess who I'm with, honey? The FBI!

You'll never believe what happened. My car was impounded.

The cops think we killed Gianna.

I rewrite my text to him multiple times, adding and deleting information, fretting over my tone and his reaction. In the end, I opt to keep it simple and hit send before I can rethink it.

Slight hitch in our plans, fill you in later. Can you get an Uber to this address?

There's no immediate response, which isn't surprising—he won't get my text until he lands a half hour from now.

I desperately want to confer with Adele on the best strategy to explain away the journal, which, inevitably, Cho will find. No doubt, processing the car includes taking out all our luggage and going through it, piece by piece. Even a cursory glance at the journal will confirm it belonged to Gianna—there's no avoiding her name in bold on the cover.

Reed leaves the room several times, but I'm guessing we're being recorded, so I'm careful not to refer to the journal explicitly in his absence.

"I wonder if Gianna left anything behind that we missed," I say, arching a meaningful brow at Adele.

"It's not our fault if she did," she replies in an equally deliberate tone. She pulls at the ends of her hair nervously and throws a surreptitious glance at the door. "It's not like we had any reason to search the car for her stuff."

"Clay's going to be so mad when he gets my text," I say.

"He's already mad."

I pull a face. "Even madder."

"Nothing you can do about it, *now*," Adele responds.

I throw her a sharp look, picking up on her barbed tone. "Are you really going there again? I've apologized a million times. What more can I do?"

"Like I said, nothing," she says tersely.

I let out a weary sigh. I don't have the energy to argue. Adele has every right to be irritated—we could be in for a long night of questioning once the police find that journal.

I rub the tip of my finger in circular movements on the metal table in front of me. "Did you notice Reed never answered me when I asked him if CJ would get bail?"

Adele shrugs. "Do you seriously expect him to give information about one suspect to another?"

I stare at her, jaw askew. "You think he actually considers us suspects?"

"It's pretty obvious, isn't it? The FBI tracked us down, questioned us, detained us, and now they're processing your car. They wouldn't even let you pick up your husband from the airport."

Suddenly, the door opens and Reed strides back into the room. "Forensics are almost done," he announces. Neither his tone nor expression give any indication of what they have uncovered.

Despite my misgivings, I open my mouth to ask if we're free to go, when my phone pings with a message from Clay.

On my way. What's going on? I'm worried.

I type back with shaking fingers. *At the police station. FBI processing the car.*

What?!! Waiting on my bag. Don't say ANYTHING until I get there.

I sigh as I click out of the APP. I'm not sure why he bothered checking a bag—not that it matters now. We won't be going anywhere any time soon.

Reed raises a questioning brow. "Everything all right?"

I grimace. "That was my husband. As you can imagine, he's not too happy. Are we free to go after this? We need to get on the road ASAP. I have to be in New York for a meeting the day after tomorrow."

"Cho will be in to brief you in a few minutes," Reed says noncommittally. He pushes a pad of paper and a pen across the table to me. "I'll need the address you'll be staying at in New York."

I'm about to object, but think better of it. I have nothing to hide from the FBI. If Reed wants to verify my story, it will only confirm that I'm being honest with him. I scribble down my grandmother's address and hand it to him.

He throws back the last of his coffee, squeezes the paper cup in his fist and gets to his feet. "I'll bring your husband straight through once he gets here," he says, tossing his cup in the trash can on his way out.

The next time he returns, he's accompanied by a frazzled-looking Clay. I know he said he's been up 'til the early hours studying every night since I left, but I'm still shocked at his chalky complexion and the gray shadows beneath his eyes. I feel terrible knowing he's going to have to postpone his CPA exam now, on top of everything else. I don't even know if he'll have a job to go back to after this. My eyes glaze over as I contemplate the nightmare I've dragged my best friend and my husband into—a nightmare that's growing deadlier the farther east we drive.

"Are you okay?" Clay asks, sinking down next to me in the plastic chair Reed slides over next to mine.

"I'm fine," I say, the words sticking in my throat.

He presses his lips to my forehead, but not before he looks daggers at Adele. "Thanks for nothing. Hope you're happy now."

"This isn't her fault," I protest. "I'm the one who insisted on giving Gianna a ride. Adele didn't want any part of it. She tried hard to dissuade me."

"Not hard enough, apparently," Clay grumbles. "She was supposed to talk you out of making this trip to begin with."

Reed clears his throat and slides a color photograph of CJ and Gianna across the table to Clay. He taps a finger on it. "Do you recognize either of these people?"

Clay frowns down at the photo for a long moment and then shakes his head. "Is this ... the girl?"

"Yes. That's Gianna Halstead and her boyfriend, CJ Phillips," Reed confirms.

Clay's throat bobs as he swallows. "How did she die?"

A sharp knock on the door grabs Reed's attention before he can answer.

Agent Cho enters the room, a file folder and a padded envelope tucked under his arm. "Forensic techs are done with the car."

I squeeze my eyes shut and take a deep breath. My eardrums vibrate with the pounding of my heart as I wait for him to divulge that they've found the journal.

"Good! I take it we're free to leave now?" Clay says, getting to his feet.

"Yes. The car's clean," Cho confirms. "We did find some strands of dark hair behind the rear seats, but that's to be expected if Gianna was hiding back there. We're running some DNA tests to confirm they're hers."

I stare at him, confounded. Surely, he must have found the journal. Why hasn't he mentioned it? I glance across at Adele, but if she's as perturbed as I am, she's not showing it.

"We also found this," Cho goes on, reaching into the envelope he's holding and pulling out an iPad.

My mouth drops open. I turn to Adele. "That's yours, isn't it?"

"I ... I think so," she says, frowning. "Where did you find it?"

"Under the passenger seat," Cho replies.

"I feel awful for blaming Gianna for taking it," I blurt out. "But we searched the car, we couldn't find it anywhere."

Adele nods in agreement, her cheeks reddening under Cho's penetrating gaze. "I thought it might have slipped between the seats," she says. "I don't know how I missed it."

"We *both* missed it," I add, flashing her a sympathetic smile.

Clay nudges me. "We need to get on the road. We've got a long drive ahead of us."

I reach for my purse and turn to Reed. "Has CJ been charged, yet?"

He rests his elbows on the table and rubs his thumb and forefinger together, a troubled expression on his face. "We don't have enough evidence to charge him. He was released an hour ago."

My heart sinks at the news. "Can't you charge him with stalking?"

Reed shrugs. "Unless he tried to run you off the road or threatened you or something, there's nothing we can do."

I glance at Adele, but she keeps her head down, pretending to rummage in her purse for something. Clearly, she has no intention of reporting the assault. She's too scared CJ will follow through on his threat and come after us. Maybe she's right and it's better to say nothing to the police, in the meantime. There's always a chance CJ will leave us alone now that he knows we're not hiding Gianna from him. But we need to come clean and tell Clay about what happened. Since he's been dragged into the situation, it's only fair that he knows how dangerous CJ is, and that he's armed. If we encounter him again, Clay needs to understand the stakes.

Reed escorts us out to the front of the precinct where my Tahoe is parked. "Thanks for your cooperation," he says, handing me his card. "We may be in touch with you again if we have any more questions. Call me at once if CJ threatens you in any way."

I nod and mumble a goodbye, unsure what to say. *Thank you* seems inappropriate under the circumstances. I'm relieved that they're finally allowing us to leave, but it doesn't mean it's not under a cloud of suspicion.

"I'll drive," Clay says when we get to the Tahoe. I hesitate, clutching the key. It ticks me off that he thinks he's a better driver, and I'm not excited about the prospect of sitting in the back in Gianna's seat. On the other hand, I can keep an eye out for CJ's camper if I don't have to concentrate on driving, which will give me some peace of mind.

"Do you want me to sit back there?" Adele asks in a wavering tone that's begging me to say *no*.

"I'm good. You're in charge of the stereo," I answer. "I'm

going to massage Clay's neck while he drives. He looks like he hasn't slept properly in weeks."

I decide against broaching the subject of Gianna's journal until we've navigated our way safely out of the city. Clay's stressed enough about the situation, as it is. Now that I think about it, I'm relieved to be sitting behind him—this way I won't have to look at his reproachful expression when I tell him we lied to the police.

"At least that's behind us," Clay says, as he merges with the traffic on the highway and turns on the cruise control. "We can still make it to Roanoke tonight."

"We can't put it behind us just yet," I say quietly, as I begin to knead his shoulders.

"What do you mean?" Clay frowns at me in the rearview mirror. "The police might not have enough evidence to arrest CJ, but it doesn't mean they're not going to be keeping a close eye on his every move."

"Or ours," I add, my voice falling away.

"What are you talking about?" Clay asks, sounding increasingly exasperated. "The Tahoe's clean—you heard Agent Cho."

"That's what he told us," I say. "But Gianna left her journal in our car. They must have found it—they're just not acknowledging it, for some reason."

"Maybe they thought it belonged to you or Adele," Clay says.

"No chance. It had her name on it," Adele chimes in, staring out the side window.

Clay throws her a curious look. "Why's it such a big deal? Is there something you're not telling me?"

Adele turns to him, her eyes clouded with fear. "She drew this macabre sketch of us in her journal—half my brain was exposed. Next to it she'd written that one of us wasn't going to survive the road trip. Kill or be killed."

"We weren't sure if she meant CJ was going to kill her, or if she was planning to kill us," I add. "I guess we know now."

Adele shivers and rubs her arms. "She gave me the creeps from the get-go."

Clay squeezes his fists around the steering wheel and mutters something under his breath. I catch my name but nothing else.

I lean forward and prod him. "What did you say?"

"I can't believe you did something this stupid—inviting a complete stranger into your car," he fumes. "What did you think was going to happen?"

"Not this," I huff. "No one could have predicted this."

Clay gives a disgusted snort. I can feel the tension radiating off him.

"Do you think it's bad that Cho didn't mention the journal?" I ask.

"It's not good," Clay retorts. "If it wasn't important, they wouldn't be hiding the fact that they'd found it."

"The FBI aren't stupid," Adele says. "They know we had nothing to do with what happened. It's obvious from the other sketches in the journal that Gianna was afraid CJ would kill her."

I twist around in my seat and peer through the rear window at the traffic behind us. "He could be following us now. He always seems to know where we are. We searched the car for a tracking device, but we couldn't find anything —not that we really knew what we were looking for."

"Gianna," Clay mutters grimly.

"What do you mean? We checked her backpack before we let her in the car," Adele says.

Clay gives an exasperated shake of his head. "She probably had it on her the whole time."

I sink back in my seat, considering the possibility. It would explain how CJ was able to follow us all the way to Albuquerque.

But it doesn't explain how he found us after Gianna died. Unless he killed her.

23

By the time we pull up to our hotel in Roanoke, it's close to 11:00 p.m. and we're worn out from the long hours on the road spent overanalyzing our situation, while keeping a vigilant eye out for CJ's truck. I nodded off a couple of times, along the way, and woke with a start from a nightmare, certain I was tied up inside his claustrophobic camper. I can't shake the feeling that he's not done with us, yet.

We clamber out of the car and wheel our bags inside the Hampton Inn we've stopped at for the night. Clay heads straight to the reception desk to check us in, while Adele and I take a seat in a nearby lounge area. I try to make small talk with her in an effort to assuage my guilt over her being relegated to her own room tonight. It feels like I'm shoving her aside now that Clay's arrived on the scene. At first, she seemed relieved to hear he would be joining us, but now that he's actually here, I sense tension in the air between them. He's not hiding the fact that he holds her partly responsible for everything that's happened. His rationale is that if she hadn't agreed to go on the trip with me, I would have taken some anti-anxiety medication and climbed on a flight with him instead. Nothing could be further from the truth.

After brushing my teeth, I crawl into bed and pull the covers up over my head, desperate for sleep. We're planning on cutting out of here at 5:00 a.m. to make my 4:00 p.m. appointment with my grandmother's attorney. I can scarcely believe that once I sign the legal documents, he'll be handing over the keys to her house. It was a relief when Maxwell told me she'd passed away in the hospital and not at home. I'm not sure I could have stayed there knowing she'd died in her bed. Thankfully, Maxwell arranged to have the place cleaned for me, and even set up a schedule for a service to come on a regular basis until it sells.

I punch up my pillow and twist around to my other side, frustrated at how easily Clay can fall asleep. He's barely spoken to me since we got to our room. He's already asleep —or pretending to be—in the other queen bed closest to the door. I'm pretty sure he deliberately asked for a room with two queens to make a point—a petty one. He may be holding me at arm's length now, but he'll be singing a different tune tomorrow when I'm a million dollars richer. I release a heavy breath at the thought. I've imagined the thrill of signing the paperwork a thousand times since I got Maxwell's letter, but now that we're almost there, some of the joy has been sucked out of it.

Gianna's murder hangs like a dark thundercloud over what was supposed to be the adventure Adele and I would be talking fondly about well into our old age. Instead, we're going to be left trying to blot Gianna and CJ from our memories. I have to find a way to make it up to Adele. At least her iPad turned up, so that's something—I know she doesn't have the money to replace it. Maybe I'll gift her a few thousand dollars once the house sells. If she has a little cushion, it might be enough of an incentive for her to start looking for a better job, something she can be as passionate about as I am about becoming a fashion influencer.

The mood in the Tahoe is subdued when we take off for Katonah the following morning. To my surprise, Clay consents to letting me drive. He's jetlagged and wants to sleep for the first leg of the journey. There's no way he'll let Adele behind the wheel, so she's left with no choice but to get over her squeamishness and sit in the back. Suppressing a yawn, I slide into the driver's seat and turn on the ignition. I could use a serious shot of caffeine to jumpstart my system. The coffee in our hotel room tasted like dishwater, and the powdered cream they provided wasn't much better than ground up chalk. Still, it will have to suffice until we stop for breakfast in a couple of hours. Hopefully, my music playlist will be enough to keep me awake until then. The minute Clay puts in his earbuds and closes his eyes, I connect my phone to the car stereo and select *Road to Nowhere* by Talking Heads. I sing along softly, checking the rearview mirror every so often in the hope that Adele will join in, but she just stares out the side window with a frosty look on her face. Sighing, I turn the music down and glance back at her. "Are you okay? I know this isn't ideal."

She shrugs. "I'm tired of being in this stupid car, that's all."

I suck on my bottom lip for a moment, trying not to take it personally. I have to think about it from Adele's point of view. This entire trip has been a test of endurance for her. She's had her brother's ongoing issues to deal with, she was forced to endure Gianna's company against her will, she was assaulted by CJ with a deadly weapon, and now that Clay's joined us, she's stuck feeling like the third wheel again. It's no wonder she's had her fill. "If you want, I can book you a flight back home out of New York," I offer. "You don't have to drive the whole way back with us." As soon as the words leave my lips, I realize how insensitive it sounds.

"You can tell me outright if you don't want me in the car," she replies testily.

"It's not that," I assure her. "I just don't want you to feel like you're stuck with Clay. I know this isn't how you pictured things."

"We'll see," she mutters, before turning to stare out the window again.

Resigning myself to the reality that she doesn't want to talk about it anymore, I turn the music back up to drown out Clay's snoring. His phone beeps with an incoming text message and I glance at it in the console. No doubt, he's got work breathing down his neck. I reach for the phone and pass it back to Adele. "Can you read that for me? I don't want to wake him if it's not important."

Adele takes the phone and taps a polished fingernail on the screen.

I tense when she suddenly sucks in a hard breath. "What is it?" I ask, dread instantly swirling in my gut. Clay texted his boss to tell him he wouldn't be in for a few days. I hope he isn't threatening to withhold his pay in retaliation or fire him. "Who's it from?" I ask impatiently.

"I don't know but, brace yourself, it's ominous," Adele warns me. "It says, *you're a dead man.*"

A wave of panic surges through me. *Dead man.* It can't be Clay's boss—he wouldn't be stupid enough to threaten an employee. Besides, Clay's bound to have his number saved in his phone. Could it be CJ? He has my number, but how would he have gotten his hands on Clay's? I throw a discreet glance across at my husband. He's sleeping soundly, oblivious to the fear trundling through my chest.

"Text them back and ask who it is," I whisper to Adele.

Minutes tick by with no response. "They're not in any hurry to identify themselves," she remarks wryly. "They know it's not Clay texting them."

"Try messaging them again," I urge.

Adele frowns. "What do you want me to say? They didn't answer the first time, repeating myself isn't going to help."

"Tell them we're going to report them to the police if they don't identify themselves. Maybe that will trigger a response."

Adele taps out another message and hits send. I hold my breath until I hear a return ping. "What does it say?" I prompt.

"*Do it*," Adele reads. "*The cops will be more interested in what I have to say*."

Bile foams at the back of my throat. I have no idea what the message means, but it's scaring me half to death. I have to find out who this person is, and whether the threat is real. "Clay! Wake up!" I hiss, leaning over and shaking him firmly by the arm.

He jerks awake and straightens up in his seat, blinking around in confusion. "Are we there already?"

"Someone's texting you," I say. "I thought it was work so I had Adele read it to me. They're threatening you."

"What?" Clay jerks around in his seat and snatches the phone from Adele's hands, his eyes glinting with anger. He scans the messages hurriedly and then pockets his phone. "It's nothing."

"What do you mean it's nothing?" I say incredulously. "Who is it?"

"Just my doofus coworker. He's ticked off that I left him hanging. He probably thinks I'm messing with him about the police so he's jerking my chain in return."

I glance at Adele in the rearview mirror. It's clear from the dubious twist of her lips that she doesn't believe him. The scary part is, neither do I. That text didn't come from work. My first thought was CJ, even though I know it's illogical. If he's going to threaten anyone, it would be Adele or me. He doesn't even know Clay. I throw a wary glance in the rearview mirror. He could be on our tail again. It's likely Gianna told him we were going to New York.

Clay gestures at a billboard up ahead. "There's a McDonald's at the next exit if you want to grab some breakfast."

It wouldn't be my first choice, but I'm growing increasingly desperate for coffee, and a raging caffeine-withdrawal headache won't do anything to lighten the mood in the car. I don't know why Clay's lying about the text—maybe he doesn't want to say anything in front of Adele, and he'll tell me what it's about later. In the meantime, it's just another thing for me to worry about.

Inside the bustling McDonalds, we order Egg McMuffins and coffee and settle into a corner booth.

"The coffee here's not too bad," I say in an overly upbeat tone to compensate for the knife-edged atmosphere between us. At this point, I just want to get to Katonah and bring this wretched trip to a close. It's beginning to feel like a party balloon that has long since deflated. Even the thought of getting the keys to the house, a few short hours from now, isn't enough to counteract the icy vibes my husband and my best friend are sending me. I munch on my Egg McMuffin, wondering if I should call them out on it. I'm not sure I can endure the next few hours in the car with both of them either ignoring me or snubbing me. I wipe my lips and toss my napkin on the table, resigning myself to hashing it out. "Look, I know you're both upset with me, and you have every right to be. But I can't go back and change any of the decisions I made. So, how about we make the best of things moving forward?"

"Easy for you to say," Adele snipes. "You're about to become a millionaire. My future looks a whole lot more uncertain. I've got to go back home and pick up the pieces. I'm up to my ears trying to keep Jackson out of jail as it is, and now I might be trying to keep myself out too. If we end up facing a trial over Gianna's murder, I'll lose my job." She gestures with her chin at Clay. "He's already lost his."

I widen my eyes and fix a questioning gaze on Clay. "Is that true?"

"Yes," he says flatly before slurping on his coffee. "My boss fired me the minute he got my text."

"Why didn't you tell me?" I throw an annoyed look Adele's way. "How come she knows about this?"

"We talked about it while you were sleeping in the back seat last night," Clay says. He sets down his coffee cup and folds his arms on the table. "That's what the text this morning was all about. My coworker's mad because my boss dumped all my work on his desk."

I stare at him, weighing his fishy explanation and finding it wanting. If his coworker was angry about the situation, he would hardly be joking around about it in the very next breath. A prickling sensation scurries over my skin. For some reason, my husband's trying to hide the fact that he's being threatened. Maybe he doesn't know who's behind it, or maybe he's trying to protect me. If he told someone at work about my inheritance, they could be blackmailing him. It could even be CJ. Gianna might have told him I had a relative who died, and he could have put two and two together. I have no idea how adept a criminal he is, but it's not hard to find out anything online nowadays. My stomach roils at the thought. It's time Clay knew how dangerous CJ really is.

"We need to tell Clay about what happened back in Memphis," I say, fixing a steely gaze on Adele. "Do you want to tell him, or should I?"

She narrows her eyes. "We agreed we weren't going to go there."

Clay looks anxiously between me and Adele. "Go where? What are you talking about?"

"CJ accosted Adele in a restaurant parking lot in Memphis," I say. "He pushed her into the Tahoe and held a gun to her stomach. He accused us of doing something to Gianna."

"What?" Clay rasps, shooting a worried glance at Adele. "Did you file charges?"

She shakes her head. "He said if we did, he would tell the police that Gianna was scared we were going to kill her."

I reach for my coffee, trying to steady the hot paper cup in my shaking hand. "CJ's dangerous. Gianna suspected he'd killed his previous girlfriend, and now she's dead, too." I fix my gaze on Clay. "I need you to tell me the truth about that text you got. Our lives could be in danger."

Clay drops his head into his hands and lets out a beleaguered sigh. "I didn't want to scare you. CJ's been calling me and threatening me too. Gianna told him about your fashion blog, and he tracked me down through your social media. He knows where we live and everything. He's convinced you're responsible for what happened to Gianna.

He said he was going to make you pay. That's why I flew out here."

I swallow the ball of fear in my throat. "Gianna predicted she wouldn't survive the road trip, and she was right. If CJ's telling you you're a dead man, you'd better believe he'll make good on his threat."

24

———————

We finally arrive in Katonah a little after 3:00 p.m. My adrenalin is spiking as I anticipate the upcoming meeting with my grandmother's estate lawyer. We've made it here safely with no sign of CJ's camper truck, the FBI, or the highway patrol. I'm taking that as a good sign that we're in the clear on both the victim and suspect fronts, at least for now.

After gassing up and picking up lattes in a nearby Starbucks drive-through, we head to the Law Offices of Maxwell Gutfeld. I'm pleasantly surprised to find that it's in a picturesque older building with gray shingle board siding—a far cry from the LA high rise office buildings I'm used to seeing in my neighborhood. I'll have to take a few pictures to post on Instagram before I leave. It's the perfect backdrop for the wide-legged fuchsia jumpsuit I've donned for the occasion. I hurriedly tidy my hair and apply some lip gloss, before heading inside. The receptionist greets us and leads Clay and I through to an airy office at the back of the building. I feel conflicted about leaving Adele alone in the foyer, but this shouldn't take too long.

A short, square-shaped man close to seventy years of age gets to his feet and shakes hands with us. "Maxwell Gutfeld, delighted to meet you both."

He gestures to the maroon-colored distressed leather chairs opposite him, and I sink down in one, grateful that my shaking legs have carried me this far.

"I must say, Cora, you look just like your grandmother, Wilhelmina," Maxwell observes, a small smile playing on his lips.

I give an abashed laugh. "Really? I never met her."

"It was her biggest regret," Maxwell says, blinking solemnly across at me. "I was her lawyer for thirty-four years, and she never passed up an opportunity to talk about you."

I try in vain to tamp down a flicker of irritation. "Too bad she didn't try to remedy her regret sooner. I have to admit, I was shocked when I received your letter. It felt a little like she was taking the coward's way out—asking for forgiveness in death. Believe me, I'd rather have known her all these years."

Maxwell tents his fingers on the desk in front of him, a twinkle in his eye. "Obstinance dies hard. I hope you're not as stubborn as your grandmother and your mother were."

Clay lets out a snort. "She got that gene."

I cut him an icy glare before turning my attention back to Maxwell. "You knew my mother?"

"I never met her," Maxwell admits. "Wilhelmina gave me a few of your mother's old letters to read. Your grandmother and I go back a long way—she considered me a confidant."

"I see," I say, settling back in my chair. I can't help wondering if my mother's letters are still in the house some-where. I've always maintained I wasn't interested in knowing anything about my grandmother, but there is a little grain of curiosity that I haven't been able to grind down entirely. "Did she leave me any of her personal possessions?"

Maxwell nods. He reaches for a file on his desk and flips it open. "She left you the house and its contents, including all the furniture, fixtures, and personal items. Everything else—namely her vehicle, a small stock portfolio, and the cash in her bank account—she left to a charity."

"Which one?" Clay asks.

Maxwell consults the file folder in front of him. "It's called Hands of Hope. It supports the single mothers of our community."

I squirm in my seat, forcing myself to keep my mouth shut. Clay shoots me a look of commiseration. I don't know whether to burst into tears or thump a frustrated fist on the desk at the irony of it. My grandmother wasn't willing to help her own daughter when she needed her most, yet she's happy to leave her money to strangers. Nothing about that makes sense. Then again, I've never heard my grandmother's side of the story, only what my mother told me. Now that they're both gone, I might never know the whole truth. I guess I should give my grandmother the benefit of the doubt. After all, anyone can have a change of heart. At least hers softened over the years.

Maxwell clears his throat and pushes some paperwork across the desk to me. "I'm sure you're eager to see the house. Per your instructions, I've hired a cleaning service to keep it up until such time as it sells. Why don't you look over the legal documents and sign them while I make a copy of your ID?"

For a long moment, I stare at my grandmother's name, *Wilhelmina Elizabeth Cleary*. Mouthing a silent *thanks* for her generosity, I sign my own name at the bottom of the paperwork.

Maxwell beams at me and shakes my hand again before passing me a set of keys. "Congratulations! You're officially a homeowner in the state of New York now. You have my phone number if you need me, for any reason. Please don't hesitate to call if you have any questions. Do you know how long you'll be in town for?"

"Only long enough to list the house—a few days, at most," I reply. "I'm hoping I can sell it fully furnished. Failing that, I'll hire an auction house to dispose of the contents."

Maxwell hands me a copy of the documents I signed and escorts Clay and me back out to the reception area. Adele stuffs her phone in her pocket and gets to her feet. I can tell by the expression on her face that something's wrong. I suspect there's trouble brewing at home again with Jackson. Maybe she'll take me up on my offer and catch a flight back to California.

"Thank you again for everything," I say to Maxwell, before accompanying Clay and Adele out to the car.

"Yay! It's official!" I exclaim, holding the house keys aloft as we approach the Tahoe.

"Picture time!" Adele says, pulling out her phone and snapping several in quick succession. I breathe out a small sigh of relief at her upbeat mood. Hopefully, we can all enjoy a celebratory dinner in a nice restaurant later on and put the squabbling behind us.

I walk around to the driver's door and come to a sudden stop at the crunching sound of glass beneath my feet. The blood in my veins turns cold when I see the smashed driver's window. There's a piece of cardboard lying on the seat with a message scrawled across it.

Told you you'd hear from me again.

25

"**C**J's here!" I manage to squeeze out.

Adele hurries over to me and claps a hand to her mouth. She takes a couple of jerky steps backward, darting an uncertain look around the parking lot. "How ... how did he find us?"

Clay immediately jogs off around the corner of the building, presumably to search for anyone lurking in the area.

My heart slugs against my chest as I scan our surroundings. We're parked in a deserted lot, shaded by mature trees, directly behind the law office. I'm pretty sure Maxwell doesn't have any cameras installed back here, so we won't have any way to prove that CJ was behind this. But there's no doubt in my mind that this is his handiwork. Nothing's been taken from the car, as far as I can tell, so the only reason he smashed the window was to intimidate us. The message he left was glaring in its intent—he can find us, anywhere.

"I didn't spot anyone skulking around or hightailing it down the street," Clay reports, when he returns, a few minutes later. He pulls out his phone and starts taking pictures of the damage to the Tahoe. "We're going to have to submit a claim to the insurance company."

"How did CJ find us back here?" Adele asks, chewing on her nail with manic ferocity.

"How do you know it was CJ?" Clay asks, surveying the damage with a pragmatic expression. "It could have been kids back here messing around."

I reach into the car and retrieve the cardboard from the seat. "He left a calling card. This is the same thing he said to us in Memphis after he assaulted Adele. He wants us to know he's here."

Clay studies the cardboard sign, his face draining of color. He throws a harried glance over his shoulder, then opens the back door of the Tahoe and starts ferreting around in his bag.

"What are you doing?" I ask.

"Making sure we're not sitting ducks." He slams the door shut and straightens up, strapping on his gun holster.

"You brought your revolver?" I gasp, as it suddenly dawns on me why he checked his bag.

He gives a grim nod. "I packed it after CJ called and threatened me. I was hoping I wouldn't need it, but I'm not taking any chances. You said yourself he was dangerous. If he follows us to your grandmother's house, we'll need some way to defend ourselves."

Adele shuffles nervously from one foot to the other. Her eyes meet mine and I know she's thinking what I'm thinking: CJ has a gun too. This could devolve into a perilous situation. I need to try and reason with Clay—alone. Adele doesn't need to hear this. She's freaked out enough as it is.

"Why don't you borrow a brush and pan from Maxwell so we can get this glass cleaned up?" I say to her.

She gives a jerky nod and hurries off.

"We have to call the police," I say to Clay, my stomach knotting in apprehension as I watch him adjust his holster and slip his jacket on over the gun.

He runs his hands distractedly through his hair. "Why? It's pointless. We can't prove CJ was behind this. The police will treat it as vandalism and do nothing. We'll just waste hours standing around, filling out a report for no reason. Insurance will cover the damage."

"I have to notify the FBI, at least," I say, fishing in my purse for Agent Reed's card. "They told me to contact them if CJ threatened us."

Clay throws up his hands. "The FBI aren't going to waste their time on a broken window." He grips my shoulders and stares intently into my eyes. "Cora, you need to understand, no one's going to ride in on a white horse in time to save us if this lunatic attacks. The local police won't get to the house in time, let alone the FBI. We're on our own."

I bite my lip to keep it from trembling. "I'm still going to let them know that CJ's here in Katonah."

I pull out my phone and dial Reed's number, but it goes straight to voicemail. I try to keep the wobble out of my voice as I leave a brief message explaining the situation. It's all I can do for now.

Moments later, Adele and Maxwell come bustling into view. "I'm so sorry. I can't believe this happened to you," Maxwell says, sweeping his hand back and forth over his brow in a flustered fashion. "In all the years I've been in this building, I've never had any problems with vandals. All my clients park back here." He frowns and glances around. "They were certainly audacious, striking in broad daylight. I suppose I'm going to have to put a camera back here now."

"It was probably just a one-off," I assure him.

Adele finishes sweeping up the glass from the seat and floorboards, and hands the brush and pan back to Maxwell.

"Did you call the police?" he asks.

"No," Clay answers abruptly. "They'll never catch them. I don't want to waste any more time hanging around, filling out a report for nothing. We're exhausted after our drive, and we want to get to the house before dark. We'll file a claim with our insurance company."

Maxwell gives a grave nod. "Please call me if I can help in any way." He turns and walks back toward the office, shoulders hunched. I know he feels terrible about what happened, and I feel equally bad for hiding the truth from him.

"You can drive," I say, tossing the keys to Clay. "I'm too shook up."

"What's the address?" he asks, pulling out his phone.

I retrieve my copy of the paperwork Maxwell gave me and read the address off to him: "It's 2517 Forest Hill Avenue." I've looked at it so many times over the past few weeks that I should know it by heart, but I can't think straight. I'm too busy wrestling with what's happened and worrying about what might come next. CJ's not going to stop until he confronts us again, and the next time it might not end so well.

Despite the shock of knowing that CJ has followed us to Katonah, excitement begins to froth up inside me when we pull up outside a sprawling ranch house with sloping green lawns and mature trees dotted throughout.

"Wow! This place is gorgeous," Adele exclaims, as we climb out of the car. "The lot's enormous."

"I'm not so sure about that blue siding," I say with a chuckle.

"I like the red steps leading up to the front door—they're quaint," Adele says.

Clay throws a worried glance up and down the street. "The houses in this neighborhood are all spread out—one or two acre lots by the looks of things. It feels kind of isolated. Not a good thing, under the circumstances."

"Let's go inside and check out the house," I say, retrieving the key from my purse. "If we decide it's too far off the beaten track, we can always look for a hotel instead."

Clay gives a disgruntled nod. He surveys the street one last time, before following me and Adele up the path to the front door. The key turns in the lock with a satisfying click, and a ripple of anticipation goes through me as I step over the threshold. The space is appointed much as I expected—neat and clean with quality furniture that has a distinctly old-world look to it. My gaze travels slowly over the uphol-stered paisley chairs with carved backs, gilt-framed pictures on the walls, faded throw rugs, pots filled with fake flowers, and lamps with yellowing shades. A walnut credenza catches my eye and I make a mental note to take a closer look at it later—it might contain the letters Maxwell mentioned.

"Look!" Adele says, pointing at some framed photographs hanging in the hallway. "Is that your mother? She looks just like you."

I swallow back the lump that suddenly forms in my throat as I examine a picture of my mother as a young girl around nine or ten-years-of-age standing next to a red bicy-cle. She should be doing this walkthrough with me. Better still, she should have taken me to visit my grandmother years ago and repaired whatever bridges were broken.

We continue through to the kitchen, and I'm pleasantly surprised to see that, despite the old-fashioned oak cabinets and antique plates displayed on the walls, all the appliances are stainless steel and gleaming. They can't be more than a year or two old, at most. I open the refrigerator door and peer inside. Evidently, the cleaning service that Maxwell hired has dumped the contents already. "I think we should stay here," I say. "We can pick up some groceries tomorrow. That will give me a chance to go through everything and figure out what to do with it all."

Clay opens the back door at the far end of the kitchen and sticks his head out. "There's a nice big deck out here. The yard's pretty secluded though, which makes me nervous. No one would be able to spot an intruder from the street."

"The house has an alarm system," Adele says. "I saw a control panel by the front door."

Clay frowns. "If it's even working."

"Let's go check out the bedrooms and make sure the sleeping accommodations are up to par," I say.

"You girls go ahead," Clay replies. "I'm going to take a closer look at the back yard. I want to make sure it's fenced in. I'll check the alarm, too, and make sure it's working."

"Ready to explore the new digs?" I say to Adele, as I lead the way down the wallpapered hall. The first room we encounter sports a brass queen bed with a patchwork quilt in various shades of purple with matching ruffled pillows. A floral lamp globe sits atop a footed wooden nightstand. Parked in one corner of the room is a bare spindle chair—adding to the vacant feel.

"This must have been a guest room," I say, taking a peek inside the adjoining bathroom. "Yuck! I'm not a fan of the baby pink tiled walls."

"I kind of like them," Adele says. "It gives the bathroom an element of charm."

"In that case, this room's yours," I say with a shudder. "Hopefully, the other bathrooms aren't quite as antiquated."

The master bedroom is located at the far end of the hallway and proves to be surprisingly light and airy with a large bay window overlooking the back yard. The room has a more lived-in feel to it, with stacks of books and papers covering every surface. A desk in one corner overflows with curios and knickknacks. The queen sleigh bed is covered with a seafoam green comforter and turquoise sheets which makes for an eclectic ensemble—hinting at a woman with a quirky personality. That tiny thread of curiosity about my grandmother tugs at me again. When I get a chance, I'll go through the desk in this room too, and look for those letters.

"Girl! Come here!" Adele calls to me from the adjoining bathroom. "You get royal blue tile, and a shower curtain with jellyfish and sharks."

"Charming," I say, peering over her shoulder. "It's really dark in here. It feels like you're under water."

Clay appears in the bedroom doorway and rests the palm of his hand against the doorframe, exposing the gun beneath his jacket. I catch my breath, reminded that CJ has followed us here to Katonah. A shiver runs up my spine at the unsettling thought that he might be prowling the neighborhood at this very minute.

"Does the alarm system work?" I ask.

Clay rubs a hand over his jaw. "I'm pretty sure it's operational. I just need to figure out how to set it."

I raise a questioning brow. "Do you want to stay here tonight?"

"I'm not sure. Let's order some takeout and talk about it."

I let out a frustrated breath. "I'm going to bring my bag in anyway. I want to change into something more comfortable."

"Me too," Adele adds. "I'm in dire need of a hot shower."

After fetching what I need from the Tahoe, I plug in my phone to charge, and take a closer look around the master bedroom. I have every intention of getting showered up and changed, but my curiosity gets the better of me, and I make my way over to my grandmother's desk instead.

Before long, I'm immersed in browsing through the contents. I pick up a Vintage Cats desk calendar and stare at the picture on the front. A pang of sadness hits when I realize I'm looking at the date my grandmother died. No one will ever tear off another page to admire the vintage cat beneath. Salty tears burn my eyeballs. I don't know why I'm feeling this emotional about a woman I never met. I set the calendar back down and pick up a glass ring holder containing several rings. I slide one with a large oval turquoise stone onto my middle finger. To my surprise, it fits perfectly. I rub my thumb over the stone, imagining her wearing it. Evidently, my grandmother had a penchant for all things turquoise. It just so happens to be my favorite color too. Maybe I'll keep the ring—it's evidence we had something in common, after all.

I take a seat at the desk and begin pulling out the drawers one by one, losing track of time as I root curiously through them. I lift out a shoebox from the bottom drawer and flip open the lid. My heart skips a beat when I see that it's stuffed to the brim with sealed envelopes. I reach for the one on top of the pile, expecting to see my grandmother's name on the front. To my shock, it's addressed to me. I quickly grab a handful of the letters and check them. Every one is addressed to me, with my grandmother's return address in spidery script in the top lefthand corner. Shaking, I rip open a random letter.

Dear Cora,

This morning I baked lemon-raspberry streusel muffins and

pictured you licking the spoon from the bowl like your mother always loved to do as a child. I often wonder what your favorite type of muffin is, and whether you enjoy pottering around in the kitchen as much as I do. Of course I've asked you this question before, but I know you don't get my letters. Your mother doesn't want me to have any contact with you. Even though I've given up mailing them, I can't stop writing them. Every drawer in this house contains a stash of imaginary moments we've shared. I hope one day you'll get to read all about them. I wish we could have made these memories together instead. Such a terrible waste of years.

The arthritis in my fingers is bothering me, so I'll have to sign off for now. I promise to write again soon, my darling.

Your loving grandmother

I SCRUNCH the letter tightly in my fist, tears streaming freely down my face.

She did care, after all! She did want to know me.

The sound of Adele calling my name startles me, and I hastily swat at a tear dangling from my lashes. I drop the crumpled letter back in the drawer and slam it shut before making my way to the kitchen. Adele is standing by the sink drinking a glass of water, dressed in a tank and pajama joggers.

She raises her brows at me. "Aren't you going to change? I don't want to be the only one eating takeout in my PJ's."

I give a self-conscious shrug. "Sorry, I got distracted. I started looking through some of my grandmother's things."

"Well, how does it feel?" Adele asks, leaning back against the kitchen counter and waving a hand around the space. "All this is yours, now. Just like that, you're a wealthy woman."

"It hasn't hit home yet," I admit, surveying the space. "It's all been such a whirlwind. I honestly don't know how I feel about it."

"About what?" Clay asks, trundling his bag into the kitchen.

"She doesn't know how she feels about being a millionaire. Imagine that!" Adele gives a hollow chuckle. "How do *you* feel about being married to one, Clay?"

He narrows his eyes at her, something akin to a warning glance.

Adele arches a brow at him, her lips curling into a disconcerting smile. "Are you going to tell her, or should I?"

26

FIFTEEN MONTHS EARLIER

"Congratulations," I say, clinking my glass to Cora's. "Here's to the world's number one fashion influencer."

Cora gives a faux-modest laugh, her eyes sparkling with satisfaction.

I swallow the knot of jealousy sticking in my throat and peg a hollow smile on my lips. Cora always talked about getting out of her dead-end job, but everyone talks. I never imagined when she first launched her fashion blog that it would amount to anything. But she went after it with a steely determination. Now, she has over 100,000 followers and a growing number of paid advertisers. Today was her last day at the warehouse where we've both worked as administrative assistants since graduating high school. She's her own boss now, able to make a modest living from her blog—which is why we're celebrating tonight with an over-priced cocktail at my expense in our favorite bar.

I've been telling her how happy I am for her, as best friends are obligated to do, but inside I feel sick at the thought of going into the office every day without her. It feels as if she's moving on to greater things and I'm falling behind in the game of life. I know I shouldn't feel this way. She's been my best friend since kindergarten, and she's had some rough breaks too, growing up without a father and losing her mother to cancer at only fifty-three years of age. Still, most days I'd take her lot in life over my dysfunctional family.

My parents always favored my younger brother, Jackson. They spoiled him from a young age, forgoing any pretense at discipline, and now he's an uncaged monster they can't control. They're afraid of him, and for good reason. At six-foot-two, he's an intimidating force when he lashes out in anger and smashes things around the house. He started hanging out with the wrong crowd in high school in his freshman year, and it's been going downhill from there. At this rate, he's on a path to flunk out, if he isn't expelled first. He's already done a few stints in juvenile hall, and now that he's almost eighteen, the consequences are about to become a lot more serious. My parents are desperate to get him off the path he's on, and they keep dragging me into the situation, expecting me to fix everything. I'm the only one Jackson ever listens to, but even my influence is waning. Besides, I have my own life to live. Not that my parents give that any consideration. Unlike Cora, I haven't had the time to devote to a side hustle, or anything else for that matter, when I'm constantly forced to referee our latest family drama.

"Come on," Cora shouts to me over the music. "Let's find a table."

Holding our drinks aloft, we begin winding our way through the crowded bar, keeping our eyes peeled for a place to sit. We finally spot a group gathering up their purses and belongings in a booth near the back and make a mad dash over to them.

"Are you leaving?" Cora asks breathlessly.

"It's all yours," one of the women says.

They shimmy out of the booth, but just as we're about to take their places, a group of inebriated girls beats us to it.

"Hey!" I protest. "That's our table!"

A blonde with heavily coated eyelashes blinks up at me with an abashed expression as she presses a hand to her chest. "Seriously? I don't see your name on it."

The group dissolves into raucous giggles at their spokeswoman's brilliance.

"Forget it," Cora mutters. "We'll find someplace else to sit."

"Excuse me ladies," a deep voice calls to us from a neighboring booth. "We have plenty of room, if you care to join us."

Cora catches my eye and raises a questioning brow. "Want to?"

"Sure," I say, with a defeated shrug. "We'll never find another seat. This place is packed." I slide into the booth next to a good-looking sandy-haired man with piercing blue eyes. Cora shimmies in next to me, and we set our cocktails down on the table.

"I'm Clay," the man says, grinning at us. "My buddy Daniel's at the bar getting us another round."

"I'm Adele," I say, flicking my hair coyly over my shoulder. "This is my friend, Cora."

Clay gestures to our cocktails. "Is this a special occasion, or do you ladies always drink martinis?"

"We're celebrating. I quit my job today," Cora explains. "I started a fashion blog and it's finally making money."

I give a self-pitying pout. "I'm stuck working as an

administrative assistant—hoping my lucky break will come one day soon."

Clay laughs and our eyes lock. My stomach flutters. Maybe my luck's about to change in another department.

Moments later, Daniel arrives back at the booth carrying two pints of beer. "Wow," he says, stopping in his tracks and grinning broadly at us. "Clay man, I see you got busy in my absence."

After introductions, Daniel takes a seat next to Cora. He's not bad looking, but there's no chemistry there for me. My attention is firmly fixed on Clay. Those eyes captured me from the get-go, and I can tell he's interested too. I flick my thick chestnut waves over my shoulder, grinning flirtatiously at him as I reach for my cocktail.

We banter back and forth for the next half hour or so, joking around and getting acquainted. I can't believe how easily the conversation is flowing. I have a good feeling this could go somewhere.

"You ladies ready for another martini?" Daniel asks, gesturing at our empty glasses.

"Sure," I say, before Cora has a chance to decline. Our original plan was to drink a cocktail here and then go dancing at a club nearby. But things have taken an unexpected and welcome turn. I'd much rather stay here and flirt with Clay. I don't want to break the spell of whatever is blossoming between us.

Daniel gets to his feet and strides off in the direction of the bar.

"I need to use the restroom," I say, nudging Cora to let me out. "How about you?"

"I'm good," she says, sliding out of the booth. "I can watch your purse if you want."

"I'll bring it. Might need to touch up my make up," I

reply, winking at Clay as I sashay off in search of the restrooms. I wish Cora had come with me so we could have a good gossip about the guys. I want to know what she thinks of Daniel. It's so loud in here, I can't hear much of their conversation. Hopefully they're hitting it off, too. It would be fun to double date in the coming weeks if things keep moving in the direction I think they might go in.

I groan inwardly when I reach the restrooms. Just my luck there's a huge line. It's almost fifteen minutes later before I reemerge with my freshly applied lipstick. I have a good feeling this night will end with a kiss, and I intend to be ready for it. It's been ages since I've had a date. I've been too consumed with keeping Jackson out of trouble to focus on anyone or anything else.

My stomach constricts in a sickening knot as I approach the booth. Cora and Clay are huddled up next to one another, chatting and laughing, heads closer together than I'd like. Daniel has come back from the bar and is sitting next to Cora, leaving me on the outside this time. I hesitate when I reach the booth, hoping my hint will be enough to resume our prior seating arrangement, but Cora and Clay seem oblivious to my quandary. Daniel pats the seat next to him and points at a fresh martini on the table. "That's for you. I managed to make it through that rowdy crowd without spilling a drop."

I flash him a frozen smile of thanks as I take my seat. My throat feels suddenly too dry to speak. Taking a big gulp of my drink, I cast a furtive glance at Cora and Clay. What does she think she's playing at? Just because she's celebrating being her own boss doesn't mean she gets all the breaks. I try several times to inject myself into their conversation, but it's hard to make myself heard over the racket going on around me.

I end up consuming my second martini far too quickly while Daniel makes a nauseatingly heroic effort to keep up a one-sided conversation in my ear.

"Hey Addie," Cora shouts across to me. "The guys want to come to the club with us. You okay with that?"

"That's fine," I say, smiling tightly while fuming inside. I hate how Cora always makes a point of calling me Addie when she wants her way. She's stubborn enough that she usually gets it. I can't let that happen tonight. And I'm going to tell her to stop calling me Addie—it sounds so juvenile. We're not in high school anymore.

At the club, I make every effort to keep the four of us dancing together in a group, but the minute the first slow song comes on, Clay snakes his arms around Cora's waist and pulls her close. Daniel asks me to dance, and I consent —not because I want to be anywhere near him. But I need to keep tabs on Clay. I maneuver closer on the dance floor and try to catch his eye, but he doesn't even notice me.

He's too busy planting a kiss on Cora's lips.

27

I almost gagged when Cora asked me to host her engagement party—of course, I pretended to be delighted and honored like a best friend would. She and Clay have only been together for four months, but they've been inseparable ever since the first night we met. Truthfully, I don't know how I'm going to manage to keep my lips hitched up in a painful smile for the entire evening. My relationship with Cora has been strained in the past few months—the friendship winding down as her interest in me wanes. Between her whirlwind romance with Clay and her flourishing fashion influencer career, Cora barely has time for me—except when she needs something, which is why I'm stuck hosting the party tonight.

I know she's disappointed that Daniel and I didn't hit it off—she's expressed as much to us on more than one occasion. He's Clay's best buddy, which makes going out together awkward. So we don't, anymore. No one wants a third wheel, and no one wants to be one. On the rare occasion when Clay and I run into each other, we're always cordial. But I see the way he looks at me sometimes—a look that acknowledges the attraction simmering beneath the veneer of friendship. Admittedly, I'm still half in love with him, but a part of me hates him for taking Cora away from me. I wonder if he ever second guesses his choice. It's an interesting thought. The engagement party will be a good time to test the waters.

Thankfully, Clay's parents offered to pay for the party, and gave me a generous budget, so I was able to put together an extravaganza that has Cora fawning all over me.

"Adele, this looks absolutely amazing—better than I ever dreamed!" she gushes, as she walks between the white trestle tables adorned with candles on beveled mirrors and crystal bowls filled with soft pink roses. "The gold helium love balloon looks gorgeous suspended beneath the oak trees. It's so good of Clay's parents to let us use their back-yard, isn't it?"

"Uh-huh," I mumble in agreement, pretending to fuss with the napkins. Cora lucked out there too. Clay's parents are amazing people. They've embraced Cora into their family like a daughter. A pang of envy spears my heart. It hurts to think that they could have been my in-laws—it should have been Cora setting up this party for me.

"Leave the napkins. They look fine," Cora says, grabbing my hand and dragging me away from the table. "It's time for us to get dressed."

I suppress a discreet smile as I follow her into the house. We went shopping together for dresses several weeks back. Cora ended up selecting a soft flowing romantic pink sheath. It's pretty in an understated sort of way, but chaste enough for the in-laws to approve of. I purchased a similar dress in blue but, unbeknownst to Cora, I exchanged it a couple of days later for something with considerably more sex appeal. I want to make sure Clay knows exactly what he's missing out on. Cora is cute, as petite blondes go, but she doesn't have curves in all the right places, and I intend to highlight our differences this evening.

I get dressed in the bathroom before joining her in the guest bedroom where she's applying her makeup at the dressing table.

"Wow!" she says, blinking at me as she tries to mask a disapproving expression. "What happened to the dress you bought at Nordstrom?"

"I'm such an idiot," I say with a glum sigh. "I took it out to iron it and accidentally burned it. I had to rush all over the place yesterday trying to find something else to wear at the last minute." I smooth my hands down the red satin fabric trying to look more stricken than smug. "Hopefully, this will do," I say.

"Uh, yeah, it's fine," Cora says dubiously.

I turn away to hide the grin spreading over my face. Fine is an understatement—I've totally upstaged her. The lace bodice and spaghetti straps do an outstanding job of showcasing my best assets. And the flirty open back and side slit hint at just enough skin to draw in a roving eye. It may be Cora's engagement party, but it will be Clay's last chance to get a good look at what he's passing up.

Before long, the party's in full swing. Cora is soon swept away in the excitement of the games and gifts, and has forgotten all about my dress. But I can tell by the glances I'm getting that it hasn't escaped everyone's notice. I even stoop to flirting with Daniel in Clay's vicinity to make sure he gets an eyeful. He tries to be discreet about it, but I catch him looking my way multiple times over the course of the evening, and when our eyes lock for a moment too long during a game of Wedding Movie Charades, I have my answer.

Clay is second guessing his choice.

28

Standing next to Cora at the altar on her wedding day in my dusky lavender bridesmaid's dress, I catch Clay's gaze traveling over me. A tingle of excitement shoots through me at the unmistakable look of longing in his eyes. I flutter my lashes, outwardly demure, inwardly hiding a forbidden secret. We shared our first stolen kiss the night of the engagement party. Clay's parents graciously invited Cora and me to sleep over in their guest house so we wouldn't have to drive home after consuming copious amounts of champagne. Cora had already gone to bed, but I hung around outside helping Clay take down decorations and stack chairs for the rental company to pick up in the morning. We were standing under a Bride and Groom banner at the bottom of the garden, discarded tulle and tangled fairy lights strewn at our feet, looking all the world like the happy couple, when he suddenly took me in his arms and kissed me—a kiss that was filled with equal measures passion and desperation. "It should be you, Adele," he whispered in my ear. "It's you I want."

A day or two of guilt, solely on his part, followed, and

then it happened again. As the guilt waned and desire grew, we began to plan our first overnight rendezvous. Clay told Cora he had a business trip, while I was purportedly at my parents' place dealing with another Jackson-related drama. After that first weekend, we became increasingly creative in dreaming up covert ways to meet—early morning get-togethers, extended lunches, and the like. We even bought burner phones so we could text and call each other freely without fear of being discovered.

I stare down at the peony-and-rose bouquet I'm holding in my hands as I relive the thrill of countless illicit late night phone calls. I'm only half-listening to the preacher as Clay and Cora exchange their doomed vows and slide shiny new wedding bands onto each other's fingers—a circle of fraud, Dante's eighth circle of hell. But Clay won't be trapped there for long. I'm already dreaming of what lies ahead—a future where I'm no longer the unwelcome third party.

I'm vaguely aware of the minister telling Clay that he may kiss the bride, as the crowd erupts in euphoric applause. I cement my lips into a smile to appease the photographer buzzing around the bridal party—not that it matters. The photographs documenting this day will be discarded like a bad memory, all too soon. I wish the day didn't have to go forward at all, but Clay made me promise to grit my teeth and bear it, with the understanding that he would file for divorce within the year. Despite doing every-thing in my power to talk him out of this sham marriage, he felt duty bound to go through with it. He got swept along in Cora's elaborate wedding plans, generously financed by his parents, and couldn't back out at the last minute. They had put non-refundable deposits on everything, and his moth-er's side of the family in Australia had already bought their plane tickets.

I steel myself to look euphoric as I link arms with Daniel and follow the bride and groom down the aisle. The whole scenario feels staged—as though we're actors on a movie set. I can't help thinking that any minute now the director will call "Cut!" and Clay will break away from Cora and come running to me, declaring his love for me in front of everyone. But when I see Clay's mother dabbing her eyes as she embraces him, I realize that's not going to happen today. The lines between reality and fantasy are beginning to blur in my brain. I want to shout out over the crowd that it's me Clay's really in love with, but I know I need to stick to the script and keep smiling through the rest of this evening, and over the coming weeks and months. It seems like an eternity stretching out before me.

Clay keeps telling me I need to be patient, but it's hard to be patient when you feel like you have a hot blade twisting in your heart. I won't wait forever.

29

___

lay was on board with everything, until the day the letter arrived from the law office. That glossy envelope—his golden ticket to a fortune. I still remember how luxurious and velvety it felt in my hands when Cora showed it to me. That's the day I snapped inside. It was the last straw. Cora already had everything, and she'd taken everything from me. By then, her income from her fashion blog had eclipsed my paycheck by a wide margin, and now, with the inheritance to boot, she would have more money at her disposal than either of us had ever dreamed of. Right away, she began making plans to buy a house and start a family. "There's no reason to wait any longer!" she told me excitedly. "We can afford a baby now!"

I spent days stewing about the situation. I could tell Clay was getting cold feet when it came to divorcing Cora. It's funny what money will do to a person. At that point, I had very few cards left to play, so I played the only one I could. I stopped taking the pill. I had to beat Cora to it. I thought for sure Clay would choose me over her when I told him I was pregnant. But, to my dismay, it only made him dig in his heels. He told me in no uncertain terms that it was over. He didn't want to entertain any discussion about it, and he didn't want to see me anymore. He stopped responding to my texts and taking my calls. That's when I agreed to go on the road trip with Cora. I knew it would give me leverage over Clay. He was nervous about my intentions, wondering if I would tell her about the affair, fearful that I might harm her.

The truth is, I wasn't sure what I would do.

30

PRESENT DAY

"What's wrong, Clay?" Adele simpers. "You look a little tongue-tied all of a sudden. What about the part where you wanted to be the one to tell her?"

I blink in confusion, my eyes darting between Adele and my husband as I wait for him to say something. I can't make sense out of Adele's incoherent prattle. Why is she acting so strangely? And why the scathing questions about how it feels to be a millionaire, or to be married to one? Apparently, she's been harboring more jealousy toward me than she's let on. What hurts the most is that it sounds as if she and Clay have been talking about my inheritance behind my back. Maybe Clay has even confessed to feeling somewhat emasculated, knowing I was about to become heir to a boatload of money. But every time it's come up in conversation, I've always taken pains to assure him that it's our money, to build our future and our family.

"That's enough, Adele," he says at last, in a tone I don't quite recognize—overly controlled, in a vaguely threatening kind of way. I suck in a breath when I see his fingers surreptitiously slip inside his jacket. Is he reaching for his gun? I open my mouth to say something, but my throat feels as if it's been sealed shut, and I can't force the words through.

Adele presses her lips into an annoyed grimace as she tosses her curls over one shoulder. "Fine! If you're too much of a coward to tell her, I will."

"No! Wait!" Clay blurts out. He takes a step toward her, but she holds her palms up to him. "Too late! You had your chance—plenty of them, if we're being honest. We're running out of time. I'm going to handle this now."

She swivels to face me, a Narnian coldness to her features that takes my breath away. Her eyes bore into me, glittering ice chips of disdain. "Your husband was supposed to be the one having this conversation with you, but he's too spineless to see it through. So I'm going to do his job for him. There's no easy way to tell you this, so I'm just going to lay it out for you—Clay and I are having a baby together." She glances at him, a twisted smile of satisfaction on her lips, before turning back to me. "We're planning on getting married as soon as he divorces you. That's why he keeps putting you off every time you broach the topic of starting a family—he's already started one with me." She laughs, and the sound scrapes over my heart like fingers of steel. "I didn't want to tell you here in your new house, but you have your soon-to-be-ex-husband to thank for that. He got cold feet about telling you he was going to be a father when he heard about your inheritance. He wanted to get his hands on some of the money first. Pretty shallow, don't you think?" She cocks a brow, inviting me to respond.

I blink at her, feeling like I've stepped into some kind of alternate reality. I try to form a response, but my lips have turned to rubber. I grab the kitchen island to steady myself and sink down on a rattan bar stool. The look on Adele's face is so sharp and scathing, it pierces me to my core. I can't figure out what's going on with her. Is this some kind of horrible joke? I know she's been under a lot of stress lately, and she feels left out now that Clay and I are married—jealous even—but this is seriously twisted.

"Tell her to stop, Clay," I say weakly. "This isn't funny."

A ticking time bomb of silence descends as I wait for him to deny Adele's preposterous claims, to say something that will put this right, or to burst out laughing and tell me it's all just in jest. To my horror, he hangs his head and rubs a hand over his brow. "Believe me, Cora, this isn't how I wanted you to find out. It's all been a terrible mistake."

"Mistake?" My voice sounds piteous and thin, more like a bleat from a lamb than the cry of a scorned woman. I feel sick to my stomach and I'm dimly aware of the oak cabinets beginning to spin around me. My grip on the counter tightens.

"I told her it was over, but she wouldn't stop calling me," Clay goes on. "She's been harassing me throughout your trip, pretending it was her parents any time you walked in on her. She wanted me to tell you about the baby. She kept threatening to tell you herself. It's been a nightmare. It should never have happened to begin with."

Adele juts her chin out at him. "But it did. And now you need to choose who you're going to spend the rest of your life with—me and our baby, or your wife, in a marriage you admitted was a sham from the very beginning. It was me you really wanted. You told me that when you kissed me the night of your engagement party."

"I don't remember saying that!" Clay growls, his face reddening. "I said you were a mistake."

"Liar!" Adele spews at him.

Clay shakes his head slowly. "You need to face it, Adele. It's over. I choose Cora."

For a frozen moment, they glare at each other, and then everything begins to move in slow motion before my eyes. Adele lets out a maniacal shriek and lunges at Clay. Too late, I detect the glint of a blade in her hand. My heart convulses when I realize she's grabbed a knife from the block on the counter. I leap from the stool with outstretched hands as if, by some miracle, I could stop her in the nick of time.

"Wrong choice!" she screams, thrusting the knife into Clay's stomach. He lets out a grunt, before crumpling over and falling to his knees.

"Wrong choice—just like the night we met," Adele hisses in his ear. "You should have picked me."

31

"Clay!" I yell, flinging myself across the floor in a desperate bid to reach him.

In one swift move, Adele wrenches the revolver from his holster and tosses the bloodied knife into the sink. She swivels and points the gun at me, her lips set in a grim line. "Now, neither of us can have him."

"Who are you?" I croak, scrambling backward. "I don't know you anymore."

She laughs. "That's an understatement! You've been so wrapped up in your Vogue mania for the past year, you don't even know your own husband. What a waste! Thankfully, I was there to pick up the pieces and show Clay what a real relationship looks like."

I give a bewildered shake of my head. "Why are you doing this? I thought you were happy for us. You planned our engagement party. You were my maid of honor at our wedding!"

"You ... took ... him ... from ... me," Adele snarls, dragging each word out like a roll of barbed wire. Her eyes narrow. "It was me Clay wanted the night we met in the bar. He chose to sit beside *me*. We hit it off right away. Everything was going great, right up until I left to go to the bathroom. Then, you sidled into my spot, like the snake you are, and left me stuck talking drivel with Daniel for the rest of the night. You ended up with Clay because you orchestrated it. Not because he chose you."

My brain reels as I try to digest what she's saying. I remember sliding into the booth, when Adele and Daniel took off, but only to make myself heard over the music—not in some underhanded attempt to switch seats. We'd only just met the guys. How can she possibly think I stole Clay from her? I realize now, too late to rectify things, that her jealousy has been festering below the surface all this time, driving a wedge in our friendship. I throw a troubled glance at Clay. He's moaning as he holds a hand to the wound in his stomach. Does he really regret marrying me? There must be some truth to what Adele's saying if they've been carrying on an affair behind my back ever since the engagement party. All those long nights at the office at the behest of Clay's boss made for a plausible cover. I never doubted him—I was too busy juggling everything that was going on in my fashion world. Tears cling like film to my eyeballs as I fight to keep them from falling. Is Clay in love with Adele? I suck in a sharp breath when I notice the blood seeping through his shirt. Wherever the truth lies, I can't dwell on it now. He's going to die if I don't do something.

"Please," I plead, my voice catching in my throat. "Let me help him."

Adele gestures with a wave of the gun at his hunched figure. "Knock yourself out. There's nothing you can do for him now. He's paying the price for the choice he made. It has to be this way." A shadow flits across her face, lending her features a macabre air. "Jackson makes a lot of bad choices, and my parents never force him to face the consequences, and look where that's got them. Men need to learn there are consequences. They don't get to walk away. They can't be allowed to take advantage of the women in their lives—like CJ did with Gianna." She stares at me, her pupils dilated with a semblance of madness. "Clay took advantage of your naiveté—don't you see that? Don't you want him to be punished for it?"

I give a jerky nod, fearful of triggering her fury while she's waving the gun around. The last thing I want is for her to empty a round into me, too. I need to stay alive if Clay has any chance of making it out of here and getting the help he needs.

"No wonder your husband tired of you so quickly," Adele continues. "You never paid him the attention he craved. Go on then! See if he has any last words for you."

Cautiously, I crawl across the floor to Clay and slip my arm around his shoulders. He's still clutching his stomach in a bid to stem the bleeding, but the color is rapidly draining from his face.

"It's going to be all right," I assure him, my words ringing hollow in my ears. Up close, it's obvious his injury is severe. He needs an ambulance, and time is not on his side. With my phone still charging in the bedroom, his only hope is if I can convince Adele to call for help. I reach for a dish towel hanging from the oven door and press it to his stomach before turning back to her. "I'm begging you, please, Adele. We need to get an ambulance here now. He's bleeding out."

"There is no *we* anymore," she says, narrowing her eyes. "You sidelined me a long time ago, and now Clay's trying to do the same thing. Look at him! He's willing to die for a marriage he doesn't even believe in—all for the money.

What a fool! Too bad he'll never get to spend it, or meet his child."

Instinctively, my eyes travel to her flat stomach. I never suspected for a moment that she was pregnant. She hasn't been throwing up in the mornings and she hasn't been eating any differently, as far as I can tell—although she did pack an inordinate amount of snacks for the trip. She could be lying about the pregnancy—using it as leverage to try and convince Clay to leave me. But I don't want to rouse her anger any further by accusing her of deceiving him. She's obviously come unhinged, and the slightest provocation could end with her putting a bullet in me. I need to do everything in my power to keep her calm until I can figure a way out of this mess. "How far along are you?" I ask, willing my voice into neutral.

Her lips curve into a cunning smile. "Ten weeks tomorrow. We have an ultrasound scheduled to find out the baby's sex. Clay wants a son, you know." She casts her eyes over him in a disparaging manner. "A daughter wouldn't be good enough for him. He's just like every other man alive—he thinks women are there to be used."

I don't contradict her, but she's dead wrong on that. Any time Clay and I talked about kids, we always agreed that we didn't care if we had boys or girls. Still, it's safer to entertain her delusion than cross her in any way while she's waving a loaded weapon at me.

"I'm ... sorry, Cora," Clay wheezes. "This is why I didn't want you to take her on the road trip. I was ... afraid she would hurt you."

Adele throws back her head and cuts a harsh laugh. "Hurt your chances of getting your hands on her money, you mean." She lowers the revolver and leans back against the kitchen counter, fixing a caustic glare on me. "Don't believe his lies. He didn't want anything to happen to you before you signed that paperwork, but he was planning to divorce you afterward. He'd already looked into ways of moving half the money into another account. Bet you didn't know about that either."

I recoil from Clay's dead weight slumped against me, the life slowly leaving his body as it has our sham of a marriage. I've lost all faith in him as a husband, but I loved him once —I can't let him die here on the floor like a dog. "Why did you have to stab him?" I rasp.

Adele smirks. "I wanted him to acknowledge that his marriage was a mistake. I wanted to hear him say that he chose me instead of you, but he's still too cowardly to do it to your face. Although, he was happy enough to whisper it to me behind your back. You married a cheater and a coward. How does that feel?"

Ignoring her taunts, I open my mouth to beg her once again to call for an ambulance but freeze at a loud crash coming from outside the house.

Seconds later, the door to the deck bursts open and CJ storms through. He stands at the far end of the kitchen, legs astride, aiming a gun directly at Adele.

I suppress a scream as I tighten my grip on Clay. My heart's pounding so hard, it feels as if my chest is about to split open. I try to make myself as small as possible, shrinking back against the cabinets. There's no hope of talking my way out of this standoff. One wrong move and we'll all die in a hail of bullets.

Adele looks oddly calm as she faces off with the man who held a gun to her stomach only a couple of days earlier. I wouldn't be so confident if I were her. CJ's a hardened criminal. She's only a woman scorned, my former best friend coming unglued. I need to put an end to this now before she gets us all killed. Summoning my courage, I sit up and address CJ head on. "Please help us. My husband's been stabbed. He needs an ambulance."

CJ casts his eyes fleetingly over Clay slumped on the floor next to me. He gives a scathing snort. "I'm over him."

I frown, trying to make sense of his odd response. What does he mean *he's over him*? He doesn't even know Clay.

Adele gives a malicious chuckle. "She has no idea, CJ. It's been quite the day full of shocking revelations for her so far. Why don't you enlighten her?"

"First, you're going to tell me what you did to Gianna," he replies through gritted teeth.

Adele sighs. "Must I be the one to fill Cora in on *every*thing?"

"What are you talking about?" I interrupt. "Do you two know each other?"

"We do now," Adele spits out. "Your scumbag husband hired CJ and his loser girlfriend to follow us across the country to make sure his investment was safe. How touching! He didn't care much about *my* life though, did he? He let a loose cannon with a criminal record hold a gun to my stomach—to our baby. That's why I put a knife in him. Clay didn't care if I lived or died, why should I care about him?"

I shake my head in bewilderment. "Adele, think about what you're saying. Do you really want the father of your child to die?"

"He has to be punished," she plows on, unabated. "He lied to you. You were right about the tracking device—he put it on the car before we left so CJ could follow us. He admitted it to me while you were in your room going through your grandmother's things."

My jaw drops as I look to CJ for confirmation.

He scowls but says nothing.

Adele lets out a snort. "I guess Clay didn't know about CJ's criminal record. He and Gianna were trying to blackmail him. One way or another they wanted a piece of your money."

"Forget the money!" I say. "I'll give you both whatever you want. Just call an ambulance. If Clay doesn't get medical attention soon, he's not going to make it."

"Clay lied to me too," Adele continues undeterred. "He looked at me with those piercing blue eyes and told me to my face that he knew marrying you was a mistake the minute he saw you walking down the aisle. The whole ceremony, he was imagining it was me he was exchanging vows with. Well guess what? That mistake is going to cost him."

My gaze travels briefly over Clay's glistening features. So familiar and yet, so foreign. I guess I never really knew him, after all—never took the time. It was such a whirlwind engagement and wedding, fueled by the staunch enthusiasm of Clay's parents, eclipsed by our hectic careers. His eyes have drifted closed now, but he's still breathing, his skin a ghastly shade of gray beneath the sweat. "Clay," I whisper. "Is it true? Did you hire CJ?"

He gives a weak nod. "He's a cousin of one of my coworkers. I made the mistake of telling him about the inheritance."

"He's an out-of-work, pot-smoking loser who got kicked out of his apartment," Adele cuts in. "Exactly the kind of underachiever with enough time on his hands and insufficient funds in his bank account to drive a camper across the U.S. stalking us."

"You knew about this?" I say incredulously. "This whole time you were only pretending to be scared of the camper truck following us."

Adele grimaces. "I was in the dark, at first. I didn't know

anything about it until I spotted Gianna texting on a phone outside our hotel in Albuquerque. I knew something was up. I was beginning to think by then that Clay had put a tail on us, and I wondered if she was involved somehow. Later that night when you fell asleep, I went next door and confronted her. She admitted everything, but she was a cocky little thing. She threatened to tell you about the affair. She wanted money in exchange for keeping quiet. I gave her all the cash I had and told her to pack up and leave. She texted CJ to pick her up near the hotel."

"I got the text," CJ growls. "But she never made it."

"Obviously." Adele says coldly. "Because you killed her."

"I loved her!" CJ snarls. "But you didn't like her from the get-go, did you? She interrupted your plans. You didn't want any witnesses in the car. You were threatening Clay the entire trip. You kept telling him something might happen to Cora, if he tried to break off your relationship."

"I had to say what she wanted to hear so she wouldn't hurt you," Clay rasps. "I promised her we'd tell you together once you got back from New York." He moans softly and his head lolls to one side. He's growing weaker by the minute. I can't obsess about what he's done to me, soul-destroying as it is. I need to get him help before it's too late.

"Can't you see he's dying?" I yell. "You have to call 911. Now!"

"Not until we're done here," CJ replies, his eyes never leaving Adele's face. "Not until she confesses."

She stares back at him, unperturbed. A curious smile sculpts her lips. "How does it feel to face a woman you can't control, for once?"

"It doesn't look like you're in control," CJ replies drily. "Sounds to me like you got dumped."

Adele's face contorts. Without warning, she raises Clay's

revolver and pulls the trigger. CJ stumbles sideways, but not before returning fire.

"No!" I scream, watching in horror as Adele collapses to the floor. The revolver slips from her hand and skids beneath a nearby cabinet. CJ limps across the floor to her. He doesn't appear to be badly injured—a flesh wound, most likely. I gasp aloud when he picks up Clay's revolver and holds both guns over Adele's head, execution style. "Last chance for a confession. What did you do to Gianna?"

"CJ! No!" I yell, leaping to my feet. "She didn't kill Gianna. She shouldn't have kicked her out of the hotel—I didn't know about that. You have every right to be angry with us for abandoning Gianna, but Adele didn't kill her."

He stares at me for a long moment, and then slowly lowers the guns. He limps over to the kitchen table and sinks down in a chair. I watch with trepidation as he sets Clay's revolver down on the table and spins it around menacingly. "You try. Maybe she'll confess to you," he says, resting his gun on his good leg.

I kneel down next to Adele, flinching at the sight of the blood already pooling beneath her.

"Wrong exit," she mumbles, almost as though she's talking to herself. "Recalculating."

"Where's your phone?" I whisper, discreetly patting her pockets. "I'm going to get you out of here."

"Poor Cora," she mumbles, looking up at me. "So naive."

I shiver at the unsettling look in her eyes.

She beckons me closer, and I put my ear to her lips.

"I had to do it."

ausea roils in my stomach. *Had to do what?* Is she talking about stabbing Clay? She didn't want me to have him if she couldn't either. But there's no way she can justify her actions. No one compelled her to pull that knife on him.

"I had to kill her," she wheezes.

My lips part in silent shock. I stare in disbelief at my best friend since childhood, wondering if I heard her right. Does she mean Gianna? But she didn't kill her. CJ did. She must be hallucinating. She's lost a lot of blood— she's likely mixing up snippets of conversation in her mind.

"Ssh!" I whisper. "You don't know what you're saying."

"I'm dying. There's no need to hide the truth any longer. I killed Gianna."

I shrink back from her and press my fists to my mouth. *Please, don't let this be true.*

"She wanted more money," Adele goes on. "I told her I didn't have any."

"You should have come to me," I say, choking on a sob. "We could have figured something out together."

Adele gives a hollow laugh. "Not the kind of money she was talking about. She got greedy. She wanted me to help her and CJ kill you once the house was in your name. She knew Clay would inherit everything. She and CJ were planning to make him pay up."

"You lied about seeing her in Memphis," I say in a half-whisper, as my mind rewinds through the past few days, trying to untangle the truth from fiction.

She lets out a mirthless laugh. "I had to do something to put you out of your misery. You were so worried about her. I destroyed her journal too. I couldn't risk it being used against us."

"What's she saying?" CJ calls over to us.

"Nothing. She's just rambling," I reply over my shoulder.

He gets to his feet with a grunt and hobbles back over, glaring down at Adele. "Time's up. Are you ready to confess?"

She stares back at him, her eyes cold and emotionless.

Without warning, he swivels and levels the gun at my head. "Maybe this will help grease your lips," he growls.

Adele moans and struggles to sit up. "Leave her out of it. This is between you and me."

"I'm out of patience and you're out of time," CJ says, pressing the cold barrel of the revolver directly into my temple.

"Okay! Put the gun down," Adele wheezes. She leans back against a closet door and lets out a tremulous sigh. "I followed Gianna when she left the hotel. I went out a side door to avoid the cameras. I wanted to confront her about blackmailing me. I had to make sure she got the message that there wasn't going to be any more money." Adele wets her lips before continuing. "She wouldn't back down. She was irate. She came at me with a rock. I wrestled it out of her fist and struck her on the head with it. It was all over before I had time to think." Adele shuts her eyes and exhales a shuddering breath. "She dropped to the ground instantly. I couldn't revive her—believe me, I tried."

"So you threw her behind a dumpster—discarded her like a piece of trash?" CJ bellows, reaching down and grabbing Adele by the throat. "That's all she was worth to you?"

Adele makes a gurgling sound, one hand swatting helplessly at CJ's iron grip.

I curl my hands into fists, wondering if I can manage to overpower him before he shoots me. He's so consumed with hatred for Adele, he seems to have momentarily forgotten I'm here. I have to do something before he kills her. Silently, I get to my feet, pad quietly backward, and reach for Clay's revolver lying on the table. "Let her go!" I scream, aiming the gun at CJ.

He whirls around, his face distorting in rage, but, before he can react, a commotion at the back door distracts us both.

"Hands in the air!" a commanding voice booms out. "Drop your weapons!"

My eyes widen as a bevy of uniformed police officers spill through the door in a blur of blue, guns drawn and ready for action. Gingerly, I lay Clay's revolver at my feet and raise my hands in the air. I'm shaking from head to toe, a powerful combination of fear and relief surging through my veins. I don't know how the police found us, but I couldn't be happier to see them. I glance over at CJ, relieved to see that he has his hands up in surrender too. The terror inside me slowly subsides when I realize the terrifying showdown is finally over.

Within minutes, the kitchen fills up with bustling paramedics and before I know it, Clay is being wheeled out to a waiting ambulance.

"Can I go with him?" I ask. "I'm his wife, Cora Lewis."

"We need to take your statement first," a hollow-eyed officer with a thin mustache replies.

I give a jerky nod, watching out of the corner of my eye as CJ is restrained and led outside.

"He broke in and shot my friend," I blubber, heaving back sobs. "He's been stalking us."

"Who stabbed your husband?" the officer asks.

I swallow the knot of dread in my throat before answering. "That was ..." I turn to look at Adele, gasping at the sight of two paramedics unfolding a body bag next to her.

"Is she—" My voice trails off.

"I'm sorry," the officer confirms. "She didn't make it."

I squeeze my eyes shut to trap the torrent of tears threatening to flood my face. The breath feels like it's being sucked from my lungs. Despite the depth of Adele's betrayal, I can't help feeling that I played a role in her death. I should never have pushed her to come on this fateful trip to begin with.

The officer guides me over to the kitchen table and pulls out a chair.

"How did you know—did someone report gunshots?" I ask, sinking down in the chair gratefully. My legs feel like twigs beneath me, unable to support my weight any longer.

"The FBI notified us that CJ was in the area, possibly headed to this address. He's a suspect in his girlfriend's murder."

"He didn't do it," I croak. "It was ... an accident."

The officer raises his brows and pulls out a notebook. "You'd better start at the beginning."

33

Back in my apartment in Los Angeles, I brew myself a large mug of coffee and sit down to go through some more of the letters I discovered at my grandmother's house. There were hundreds of them stashed all over the place in every imaginable nook and cranny. I boxed them all up in plastic storage bins and brought them back to read at my leisure. I wanted to take my time and simmer with my grandmother's thoughts, in a belated attempt to get to know her.

The days following the shootings remain a chaotic jumble in my mind. I don't know how I would have got through them without Maxwell Gutfeld's invaluable assistance. I can understand now why my grandmother thought so highly of him. He proved himself to be a rock throughout—stepping in and handling as much as he possibly could for me. He even arranged for a hazmat crew to come in and clean the house after it was processed as a crime scene. Most of the contents were auctioned off last week, and the house has been listed with a competent realtor whom Maxwell recommended. The realtor tells me she expects it to sell quickly. I've listed it slightly under market value due to the fact that someone was murdered in it—an inconvenient truth that won't sit well with every prospective buyer. It doesn't sit well with me either, which is why I'd rather offload it as soon as possible, even if it means sacrificing some of the profit.

Despite everything that happened, I miss Adele. It's not easy to remove a best friend you've known since childhood from your heart and your memories—and there were a lot of good ones. I'm still not entirely sure why she did what she did. I guess they don't call jealousy a monster for nothing. Monsters can grow until they become uncontrollable and end up destroying everything in their wake. I do feel guilty knowing I was so consumed with my business that I wasn't able to be there for her when she needed me. She was under a lot of pressure from her parents to keep Jackson out of trouble, and she got little thanks for her efforts. I suppose my life seemed charmed in comparison—starting a promising fashion blog, attracting the attention of advertisers, marrying the man of my dreams who was well on his way to becoming a CPA, and then, to top it all off, a million dollars falling into my lap.

I sigh as I reach for my coffee. What hurt the most was finding out that Adele had achieved the one thing I really wanted. The autopsy showed she was indeed pregnant with Clay's child. In a sick twist, she'd managed to find a way not to be the third wheel anymore. Turns out that was me all along.

As for what happened to Gianna, I want to believe Adele's version of events. It seems plausible that Gianna attacked first, and Adele reacted. Gianna was volatile and her moods could change on a dime. She seemed to derive a certain pleasure from taunting us, and I imagine she enjoyed having the upper hand over Adele once she found out about the affair and the money at stake. I don't believe for one second that Adele confronted her with the intention of killing her. I think she snapped in the moment. She wasn't in her right mind.

CJ, on the other hand, remains convinced it was premeditated. I'm told by Agent Reed that he'll be tried for second degree murder. He appeared to be attached to Gianna in his own way, but I suspect her stories about his control issues were not entirely unfounded. Thankfully, the police managed to track down his ex-girlfriend who turned out to be alive and well and living in Las Vegas with a new partner.

I take the lid off a plastic storage tub and reach for a fresh fistful of letters. I'm gradually building a picture in my mind of the grandmother I never knew as I read through them. All these years, I was convinced she never gave me a second thought, but it turns out the opposite was true. I was her lifelong obsession. It was almost as if she was trying to be a virtual grandmother to me, documenting her thoughts and emotions, describing what we would be doing together on any given day, if things had been different. I open the first letter on the top of the pile and begin to read, quickly losing myself in an imaginary trip to the zoo. I'm touched by my grandmother's vivid descriptions of my reactions to the animals. It doesn't take long before the tears are tracking down my cheeks.

I'm immersed in perusing the letters when the doorbell rings. Draining the last of my coffee, I push the tubs to one side and make my way to the front door.

"Hi," I say, stepping aside to let Clay come in.

"Hey," he mumbles. "Doing okay?"

I stare at him until his cheeks redden. "You don't have

the right to ask me that anymore. Just get your stuff and leave."

He gives a sheepish nod and heads into the family room to begin dismantling his stereo system.

I haven't seen Clay since he was released from the hospital. His parents flew out to New York the minute the police called them. It breaks my heart to know that Clay's actions have destroyed my relationship with them. They've always been the best in-laws they could possibly have been—stepping in to fill the aching void my parents left behind. They didn't know what to say to me while we sat together in a stuffy room, waiting for Clay to get out of surgery. They were as shocked as I was by everything, unable to process it. But, at the end of the day, Clay's still their son and someone had to be there for him. Once I knew he'd made it safely through the surgery, I left him in their care. I didn't want to be there when he woke up. I couldn't give him the false hope that we would survive this as a couple. The betrayal ran too deep, shredding the flimsy fabric of our relationship.

I've already packed up all of Clay's clothes and personal items from our bedroom and moved them out into the hall. I couldn't face sleeping in there with any reminders of him. I haven't had time to tackle the rest of the apartment, yet, or the garage where he keeps all his tools and motorcycle gear. I told him he could have this morning to get all his belongings out of the apartment, and, after that, I would donate anything left behind. I have no desire to drag this out any longer than necessary. "When you're done, I have the paperwork for you to sign," I say, sticking my head into the family room.

He nods woodenly. "Leave it on the kitchen table for me."

I filed for divorce as soon as I got back to Los Angeles. I also had my attorney draw up legal paperwork for Clay to sign, relinquishing any claim on my inheritance. Thankfully, he didn't put up a fight. My attorney assured me Clay would have lost in court anyway, under the circumstances, but at least I don't have to waste more money going through the process.

For the next few hours, Clay works steadily, dismantling shelves, packing up his music gear, and clearing out the garage and the attic. I'm in the middle of making a sandwich when he comes into the kitchen, covered in dust, and sweaty. "Do you want something to eat?" I ask frostily.

He shakes his head. "No thanks. I'm just going to sign the stuff from the lawyer and get out of here."

I gesture at the air fryer on the counter that he brought home from Costco a few months back. "Take that with you, too. I won't use it."

He unplugs it, and then reaches for the pen on the table and signs his name on the paperwork without even glancing through it.

"It's not like a good CPA to skip the fine print," I say, when he hands it to me.

He gives a dispassionate shrug. "I deserve whatever's in there." For a long moment, he holds my gaze but there's no appeal for mercy in it. We both know that's not going to happen. All the lies have piled up between us like an impenetrable dam forcing our lives to divert paths.

"Anything else you need from me before I take off?" Clay asks.

An unexpected sob knots in my throat. "I just want to know why. If you wanted to be with her, why didn't you simply ask me for a divorce? Of course, I would have been hurt, but Adele would still be alive." I hesitate before adding, "And your baby."

An expression of pain rips across his features. "You were

so caught up in your work, heading off to fashion shows every weekend. I was lonely. Adele felt neglected. I was under a lot of stress at work, and she was under a ton of pressure from her family. We empathized with each other. She made me doubt what you and I had together. I began to wonder if I'd made a mistake—if I'd picked the wrong girl." He rubs a hand over his jaw. "I needed to be sure. It was selfish of me, I get that. I wanted it all. And now, I have nothing."

"You still have your family," I point out. "Your parents will always be there for you. They're good people."

He gives a thoughtful nod. "That reminds me, they want you to keep the Tahoe."

"It's very generous of them, but I'll have enough money of my own now to purchase a new vehicle." I hesitate before adding, "The truth is, I don't particularly want to keep driving it after that nightmare of a road trip."

"What about you?" Clay asks. "You don't have anyone to be there for you now."

I give a nonchalant shrug. That might be about to change, but I'm not going to ease Clay's conscience by sharing my news with him. He's not a part of my life going forward.

He turns to go and then hesitates. "For what it's worth, I'm truly sorry."

"I'm not sure it's worth anything," I reply. "Choices have consequences."

His face falls, but I can't help thinking Adele would be proud of me for standing firm.

I watch from the doorway as he secures the load in the bed of his truck with straps. When he pulls out of the driveway, he doesn't wave and he doesn't look back. I tell myself it's better that way as I blink back tears.

Closing the door on my past, I make my way back to the kitchen to eat my lunch. I've lost so many people close to me that I sometimes wonder if there's something wrong with me. One thing I know for sure—I need to get my head out of the clouds and pay better attention to the people in my life. I don't want to repeat the mistakes my mother and grandmother made. My sandwich sticks in my throat and I push the plate aside. I'm not sure what my future will look like now that all my dreams have been shattered. I don't even know if I want to buy a house anymore. It seems pointless without a family to fill it. Maybe I'll travel for a year instead —fill my fashion blog with experiences from around the world. I don't have to decide right now. For the moment, I'll keep all my options open.

Thanks to a letter I discovered in my grandmother's attic, I still have a chance at a family. My mother wrote to my grandmother shortly after I was born and mentioned my father by name. Apparently, he knew about the pregnancy and wanted to marry her, but after she fell out with my grandmother, she disappeared from both their lives without a trace. Sadly, my father turned out to be yet another family member my mother robbed me of the chance to get to know. Her pride and stubbornness ended up destroying her relationships with the people who loved us the most. I don't intend to end up in the same place where she and my grandmother were when they died—alone and filled with regrets.

I tracked down my father on Facebook and messaged him last week. I was ecstatic when he responded the very next day. He said he'd always wondered where my mother had disappeared to, and often imagined me growing up. Maxwell was wrong about my resemblance to my maternal grandmother. It turns out I'm the spitting image of my father. He's a handsome man—happily married with two grown sons, one of whom is also married and has a four-year-old daughter who specializes in playing dress up. I've seen pictures of her, and I can't wait to meet her and be the cool aunt to a next-generation budding fashionista. I need to feel like I belong somewhere. I've lost the family I dreamed of, but I can still embrace the one I've found.

My father and I are planning to FaceTime each other soon. Baby steps. I'm not so naive anymore to believe everything will work out perfectly. Relationships are as hazardous as rollercoasters—rendering the unexpected at every turn—but I'm willing to ride this one.

———

A QUICK FAVOR

Dear Reader,

I hope you enjoyed reading *Wrong Exit* as much as I enjoyed writing it. Thank you for taking the time to check out my books and I would appreciate it from the bottom of my heart if you would leave a review, long or short, on Amazon as it makes a HUGE difference in helping new readers find the series. Thank you!

To be the first to hear about my upcoming book releases, sales, and fun giveaways, sign up for my newsletter at **www.normahinkens.com** and follow me on Twitter, Instagram and Facebook. Feel free to email me at norma@normahinkens.com with any feedback or comments. I LOVE hearing from readers. YOU are the reason I keep going through the tough times.

All my best,
Norma

WHAT TO READ NEXT

Ready for another thrilling read with shocking twists and a mind-blowing murder plot?

Check out my entire lineup of thrillers on Amazon or at www.normahinkens.com.

———

Do you enjoy reading across genres? I also write young adult science fiction and fantasy thrillers. You can find out more about those titles at **www.normahinkens.com.**

THE INVITATION

*The Invitation, the next book in the **Treacherous Trips Collection**, releases November 2022.*

Accept the invitation, bear the consequences. Not everyone will come home.

Ricki Wagner and her husband, Brock, are thrilled when they get an invite to her boss's stunning lake house, never imagining the weekend of horror that awaits them. When a woman's body washes up on the sandy shore, they find themselves tangled up in a dark crime with many threads.

Everyone is a suspect as secrets begin to unravel, each one more sinister than the last. And then the texts start flooding Brock's phone—*Someone saw you, You shouldn't have come.* Ricki is already fighting for her marriage, now the truth is getting in the way.

Who can she trust when she doesn't even trust her own husband?

- A heart-racing thriller with a shocking final reveal! -

———

BIOGRAPHY

NYT and USA Today bestselling author Norma Hinkens
writes twisty psychological suspense thrillers, as well as fast-
paced science fiction and fantasy about spunky heroines
and epic adventures in dangerous worlds. She's also a travel
junkie, legend lover, and idea wrangler, in no particular
order. She grew up in Ireland, land of storytelling and the
original little green man.

Find out more about her books on her website.
www.normahinkens.com

Follow her on Facebook for funnies, giveaways, cool stuff &
more!

BOOKS BY N. L. HINKENS

BROWSE THE ENTIRE CATALOG AT
www.normahinkens.com/books

VILLAINOUS VACATIONS COLLECTION

- The Cabin Below
- You Will Never Leave
- Her Last Steps

DOMESTIC DECEPTIONS COLLECTION

- Never Tell Them
- I Know What You Did
- The Other Woman

PAYBACK PASTS COLLECTION

- The Class Reunion
- The Lies She Told
- Right Behind You

TREACHEROUS TRIPS COLLECTION

- Wrong Exit
- The Invitation

NOVELLAS

- The Silent Surrogate

BOOKS BY NORMA HINKENS

I also write young adult science fiction and fantasy thrillers under Norma Hinkens.

www.normahinkens.com/books

THE UNDERGROUNDERS SERIES
POST-APOCALYPTIC

- Immurement
- Embattlement
- Judgement

THE EXPULSION PROJECT
SCIENCE FICTION

- Girl of Fire
- Girl of Stone
- Girl of Blood

THE KEEPERS CHRONICLES
EPIC FANTASY

- Opal of Light
- Onyx of Darkness
- Opus of Doom

FOLLOW NORMA

Made in the USA
Las Vegas, NV
30 August 2022

54405799R00152